W9-CBM-301

Guelph, Ontario

This is the diary of Charlotte Mary Twiss
In which to record her thirteenth year.
Happy Birthday,
Love, Eleanor

JUNE

Monday, June 17, 1940

My 12th birthday

George phoned me long distance at six o'clock this morning to wish me happy birthday. I couldn't believe it. That is the first time anyone has ever called me long distance. I was still in bed, but he said he'd been up for hours milking the cows and feeding the chickens. I can't believe how much I miss him. He will be away working at that farm all summer and, in September, he'll be leaving home and going off to university.

I have to have breakfast now and get ready for school. I'll write more later. George did not talk to anybody but me!

Half past twelve

Before I write more about birthday things, Diary, I have something momentous to announce. When we came home for dinner at noon, Mother told us, right in the middle of passing the potatoes, that she and Dad have applied to take in a War Guest child!

Now that people think that horrible Hitler will soon start bombing British cities filled with ordinary people like us, some families are sending their children over here to be safe. And we might get one!

When Mother told us, everyone forgot it was my birthday, but I don't blame her for telling. It was too big a piece of news to keep. She and Mrs. Bennett heard about it at their WMS meeting, and afterwards she and Dad decided to apply.

Having an English child here is going to change my life totally! In this house, Eleanor and George are too old to count as children, so I am The Family Child.

Often I have wished I had a sister close to my age, someone I could play with and tell secrets to. But I never dreamed it could happen.

There is nothing else to tell about this yet. Mother said they requested a girl around my age, but we will take whoever is assigned to us. I do hope she is my age. She will live with us until the War is over! I asked how long that might be and Dad said the last war took FIVE years to finish! If this war goes on as long as that, the child and I will be practically grown up before she has to go back to England. But surely it won't last that long.

Drat. That's "The Happy Gang" song starting up on the radio. I'll have to run or I'll be late for school. NOBODY SHOULD HAVE TO GO TO SCHOOL ON HER BIRTHDAY! It ought to be against the law.

After school

All afternoon I thought about nothing but the War Child. I even forgot it was my birthday. The teacher never once noticed, but Barbara did. She passed me a note asking what was wrong with me. I guess I must have been staring into space. I explained at recess. She gave me one of her black looks. "Once she comes," she said, "I guess you won't have any time to spare for your old friends."

I told her not to be so dumb — she's the only real friend I have and she knows it. When Margaret lived here, she and Barbara and I did everything together. George used to call us the Three Musketeers. But ever since the Frosts moved to Halifax last Christmas, there are just Barbara and me.

Barbara is always getting her feelings hurt for no good reason. Mother calls people like that "thin-skinned." I call them tiresome. You have to be careful what you say to them. With Margaret, I never had to worry. If this means I am thick-skinned, I don't care.

Barbara was invited to supper tonight to celebrate my birthday, but her mother would not let her come because it is a school night. Mrs. Steiner is hard to understand. Everyone knows Barbara will be head of the class as usual. And school is so close to being over.

Barbara handed me a package when it was time to come home. I opened it then and there. It was a little statue of a fawn to put with the other animals on my knick-knack shelf. I told her I loved it and I do. It looks very sweet there next to the rabbit and the squirrel. I keep the dangerous ones like the lion and the fox on the shelf below, so the others will be safe.

But I must get back to telling about my birthday before it is over.

George's phone call was the first surprise. Then, at breakfast, Mother gave me a card he had made for me. He drew a picture of me trying to decide on my future. It has a tiny mountain climber and a doctor and a cowgirl and a professor. They are flying around over my head. Everybody laughed. I don't know how George does it.

Then Eleanor gave me this diary. Inside it she had written the words on the top of the first page about it being a diary in which I am to record "my thirteenth year." She said she thinks your 13th year is important because it is when you begin to think for yourself. I almost said that I have always thought for myself, but maybe she means a different kind of thinking. She is seventeen now, so she would know.

Then she said she realized how much I hated keeping a diary but she hoped I would try. I asked her how she knew. She said she had found some of my old diaries when she was tidying up stuff and I never wrote in any of them past the first week.

It's true. What I wrote always seemed so dull. I didn't like the way my life sounded. I feel much more interesting than that. But each blank sheet in this book looks as though it is just waiting to take down my exciting adventures. When the War Guest girl comes, we'll be bound to have some.

Anyway, Eleanor really wants me to keep a record of this year because she is sure it is going to be special and, when I grow up, I will read over this year and see myself change through the months. She also says she will give me a reward if I do it. She won't say what, but she promised it would be a good one. I actually said I would try. I wonder what sort of reward it will be. Do you suppose she has already chosen one, dear Diary?

How will I change? I cannot imagine.

Must dash — they are calling me for supper.

Tuesday, June 18, 1940

Here I am again, dear Diary. The War Guest's coming must be inspiring me. I have seen a picture of some war children in the paper but I have never met one. I wonder if they are thin and pale and nervous from living in fear.

They must worry about bombs and the Germans marching through France. Dad says the French might not be able to hold out, but maybe he is wrong. He keeps talking about Dunkirk and what a miracle it was.

I do hope that our girl is not utterly ordinary. What if I don't like her?

Oh, I will.

What if she doesn't like me?

I'll write more later. I want to read *Anne of Ingleside*. I told Barbara she could borrow it when I was done, but she mostly reads Nancy Drew. Nancy is okay, but I like other books better, like L.M. Montgomery's, for instance. I just wish Anne had not grown up so fast. I liked her best when she was a child and always getting into scrapes.

Guess what. I like reading words in a book better than writing them in a journal. Sorry, dear Diary.

After school

I was so busy celebrating yesterday that I never wrote about the other presents I got. Mother gave me a fountain pen and a bottle of blue-black Waterman's Ink and a thick pink blotter. The pen is lovely, a green Esterbrook. Fountain pens are so superior to the pencils and straight pens we use at school. It makes me feel grown-up. I already had an eraser that is half for pencil and half for ink, but ink is much harder to rub out. You end up with an ugly hole in the paper half the time. I guess I will have to be careful what I write down so I won't need to erase.

Dad gave me a dictionary of my very own, not a child's dictionary but a real one. We have the Dictionary Habit in our house. Dad has taught us to look up the meaning of each word and then read more about it. He says word roots are fascinating, and I agree. It is as though every word has its own little life story and some are old and some are just starting out.

Lizby made me a lovely cake — she may be our hired girl, but she feels like family. I got to clean out the icing bowl but did not have to help with the dishes because it was my birthday. I LOVE getting out of doing dishes, especially now that Mother has decided I am plenty old enough to wash the pots. I despise the pots. I told Lizby so. I think I hoped she would offer to do them for me, but she just looked up at me and said, "Everybody hates doing pots, Miss. Only men escape."

I got the dime in my piece of cake. It means I will be rich. Lizby got the wedding ring and Mother got the button. Lizby blushed and Mother groaned. The ring says you'll be married within a year and the button means you will end up doing housework, I guess.

When Dad got the penny he said that they would need a rich daughter to support them in their old age.

Everybody laughed but me. I hate it when Mother and Dad joke about getting old and dying. I want to have them with me always.

I wonder if our War Child worries all the time about what terrible thing might be happening to her parents. I am sure I would, in her place. How awful for her!

Dad says the people in England can have lights on as long as they have the blackout curtains pulled and no chink of light showing. After they go to bed, though, it must be pitch dark in their bedrooms with not even a glimmer of starlight coming in through the blacked-out windows. Frightening thoughts are always worst in the darkness. Mother leaves our hall light on, but in England they probably can't do that.

The War Guest's coming reminds me of Matthew and Marilla Cuthbert getting Anne Shirley in *Anne of Green Gables*. If we got a girl like Anne, it would be such fun. I do hope ours is a true kindred spirit. A bosom friend, as Anne would say.

I left out my other presents. But I need a rest. I'll get ready for bed and then come back.

Ready for bed

George's phone call was my very first present, but he left a parcel for me too. His old jackknife was in it, with a note. He said he knew I liked it and he has a Swiss Army knife now. He put in a couple more funny pictures he had drawn of me. He can sketch anything in a flash.

Lizby gave me some handkerchiefs she had embroidered, with a C for Charlotte. In the orphanage in Ireland where she was brought up, they taught the girls to sew beautifully.

Robbie Bennett brought over a box of Mackintosh's Toffee, which he got with his own money. "It is the best candy they sell," he told me.

I agree. He looked at it so longingly that I whacked the bar until it broke and then gave him a piece. It pulled out one of his teeth. He was pleased as punch, because now the Tooth Fairy will give him a nickel for it.

Aunt Carrie, who had joined us for dinner, asked him if he wasn't a little old to believe in the Tooth Fairy. He laughed and said he did not believe, but his mother did.

Everybody laughed. Then he told me that he could get an ice cream cone for a nickel at Jumbo Ice Cream downtown. Mother found him an envelope for the precious tooth and he ran back across the street to put it under his pillow immediately.

I tried to notice today whether I feel any different from when I was eleven. I don't. Maybe it takes a week or so to happen.

What if the ship our girl is on gets sunk by the Germans? It could. We hear about the ships that the

German U-boats torpedo. I must try not to think about it or I will have nightmares. I think they go for troop ships though, not ones with children.

Last bit for today

Mother found out that the Bennetts have applied for a War Guest too. They want a boy to be company for Robbie.

Eleanor asked if I'd written anything startling in you today. She was right about my not liking writing much, except writing in YOU feels different. Once I get started, words just keep spilling out.

Good night, dear Diary.

Wednesday, June 19, 1940

I was going to skip today, but Dad asked if I had written anything about Dunkirk. I do not want to but I will. It is a thrilling story. But why does it belong in my journal?

All right. I'll put it in because it is thrilling. There were thousands of British soldiers stranded on a beach in France on June 4th and hundreds of little boats that weren't Navy boats sailed across the Channel from England to rescue the soldiers before the Germans could kill them.

Fishermen went, I guess, but also other people who owned sailboats or launches. I can't imagine my family ever owning their own sailboat. But Dad says I would understand if I lived in an island country or on a coast.

The Air Force sent planes flying over, driving the Germans back until the men on the beach could be rescued. Thousands of men were there! The British kept firing at the Germans, to protect our soldiers. If it weren't for those planes, the Germans would probably have massacred the men trapped on the beach.

Dad says it was enormously brave of the people who sailed over. I couldn't picture the scene until Dad read me part of a letter he got from his friend Geoffrey Norton this morning. Mr. Norton married an English girl after the last war and lives there now. He sailed over three times and brought twelve men away. One had a broken leg and kept crying out when the sailboat bounced around in the waves.

I felt sick at my stomach before Dad finished. His voice went all husky and the letter shook in his hands. "Geoff is a lawyer, not a fighter," he said. "Try to picture Robbie's father sailing into such danger, Charlotte."

I could not do it. I suppose it is a piece of history. When children study this time years from now, maybe they will read, in their history book, about what happened long ago at Dunkirk. And I was alive for it.

I guess history is happening somewhere every day, but you don't think of it that way. It is just living.

Yet in school, History is usually so boring. Our textbook is full of pictures of old bearded men who never smile, and dates of battles, and laws. There are no girls in the history world. And I can't think of any children except the little princes in the Tower.

I wonder if my grandchildren will ask me about "the olden days" the way I sometimes ask Grandpa. I mostly ask because it pleases him, but he does have some good stories.

I can't imagine telling my grandchildren about Dunkirk. I can't imagine having grandchildren!

Thursday, June 20, 1940

I don't want to be bothered writing today. Maybe Eleanor made a big mistake getting me this diary. I never seem to be ready with all the necessary parts — the book, the pen, the blotter and ideas of things to write. I think of the ideas, but not when I am where I can write them down. I don't feel in a Diary Mood until I start writing.

Or I think of something that happened and then I'm off. This morning, for instance, Lizby woke us up screaming because a mouse ran across the floor when she came into the kitchen. When we got there, she was standing on a chair. She is so small for her age. They practically starved the children in that orphanage she came from. But she had no trouble scrambling up onto the chair. She says we need a cat, but Mother is not keen on cats.

Eleanor has this way of looking at me with her wide thoughtful eyes that makes me feel I must try harder to live up to her hopes for me. She often looks serious even when she is happy. George says she's an egghead, which maddens her. She doesn't have a boyfriend.

Maybe it is her glasses. Barbara says boys don't like girls in glasses, but Eleanor is too short-sighted to go without them. Someone should invent invisible glasses, but I am afraid there is no chance of that.

Yesterday I finished *Anne of Ingleside*. Even though she is a grown-up, Anne still has those bewitching eyes. Nobody would ever call mine "bewitching." When I stare into the mirror, my eyes just look like regular eyes staring back. They never sparkle or change colour or fill with stars. I am also too tall. Mother keeps telling me not to slouch but to stand up straight and be proud. When I stand up straight, I am as tall as she is and I feel like a giraffe.

I cannot write one more word. I'll bet L.M. Montgomery didn't write in a diary. Not when she was my age anyway. She would be out with her friends, getting into mischief.

Thursday bedtime

Diary, did I tell you that Dad tried to enlist in the Navy just after New Year's, but they would not take him because he wears glasses and is over forty and has a wife and children? He was in the last war though, right near the end. That is when he made friends with Mr. Norton who saved those men at Dunkirk. I don't want him to go this time. The very thought of my father in danger terrifies me.

But the kids at school talk a lot about whose father or brother has gone and who has not. Norma's father is in the army, training. I forget the name of the place. You would think, to hear her go on about him, that the War will be over when they see him coming. Lillian's father got turned down because of his feet. That sounded odd but she would not explain.

Barbara's cousin Daniel has signed up too, although he has not left Canada yet. He's ten years older than she is and really nice. I hope George isn't thinking of enlisting when he turns eighteen in August.

Men do look good in uniform. More handsome. Dad is not handsome really. His hair, what's left of it, is the same colour as mine. He is also a bit chubby. But he is the best father going.

Barbara came over after school and we listened to the radio and ate cookies and talked about the boys in our class. Barbara loves discussing those boys! I can't see anything so special in them, although sometimes I pretend. She brought over a new movie magazine. We took it up to my room to read. I sometimes cut out pictures of movie stars and put them up on my bedroom wall, but Barbara's parents won't let her. She hides them in her bottom dresser drawer.

Mother says those magazines are trashy and full of lies. How does she know?

My room is messy compared with Barbara's. Hers is all filled with matching pink furniture, and the ruffled bedspread and curtains are the exact same colour. I think they look babyish but I don't let B guess. She'd probably think I was jealous. None of my furniture matches, but I like it.

If only her parents didn't send Barbara to camp for the whole summer! It seems unfair. Especially when she says she does not want to go. But her mother went to that camp when she was young and that settles it. If I could go too, we would have fun. They sail and ride horses and go on overnight canoé trips. But even if we could afford that kind of camp, I couldn't leave home now anyway, not with our War Guest coming.

Last year Eleanor went to Miramichi CGIT camp on Lake Huron, between Southampton and Port Elgin. It only lasts ten days, but they have lots of fun and she's been going since she was twelve. No expensive things like sailing and horseback riding, but fun things like swimming and campfires and cookouts. They sleep out under the stars too, in bedrolls. Now I am twelve, I am old enough to join CGIT this fall. Then, next summer, I can go to CGIT camp.

Friday, June 21, 1940

I had an earache last night so I am staying home. It stopped hurting as soon as school got started, which was nice of it. I lay in bed and listened to all the soap operas on the radio. Even if you miss a month or so, nothing seems to have changed.

Mother said such a speedy cure was suspicious, but I don't think she meant it. It really did hurt in the night.

Lizby brought me a cup of tea. Her life would make a good book, Diary. Her real name is Elizabeth. When she was sixteen, she came over on a ship to help take care of a lady who was moving here. The lady went back two years later and would not take Lizby with her. Aunt Carrie heard about Lizby and brought her to help Mother care for her new baby. That was me! Eleanor was five and George was six and Mother needed Lizby badly. Lizby did not want to go back to Ireland, so she was happy to stay with us. There, that's enough for today.

Here is a thought I had, Diary. You are made of paper. Did you ever think about it? It is all made from trees. Imagine a lot of trees growing in a woods and someone tells them they are going to be made into paper. There are so many sorts of paper. Newsprint, Christmas wrapping paper, scribblers, maps, diaries like this, paper dolls, flowery notecards like Mother uses, tissue paper in dress boxes, wax paper, doilies like

Aunt Carrie puts cakes on, Dixie cups, paper towels and toilet paper! The list could go on and on. I never thought of it before, but tree careers are surprising. If I were a tree, how I would pray to be made into a lovely book and escape being toilet paper! Being a diary would be next best.

After lunch

Princess Elizabeth and Princess Margaret Rose are staying in England in spite of the War. I have a Princess Margaret Rose doll that Aunt Carrie says I am too old to play with, but I do not agree. I am not a teenager yet. I wonder if Princess Elizabeth played with dolls when she was my age. Probably not. Princesses must have to study how to be queens and don't have time to play. If the War lasts a long time, she'll grow old enough to do war work, but maybe that would be too risky. After all, she is going to be our queen someday. Margaret Rose is younger though, and she won't ever be queen.

Good thing Aunt Carrie doesn't know that I still sleep with my favourite doll Susan and that I have the others sitting in my chair. I don't really play with them now, but I tell them my secrets. They never interrupt or have to go turn the oven on or answer the telephone.

See you later, Diary.

Evening

Aunt Carrie came over today. I was in a bad mood and she said, "Keep the corners of your mouth up, Duckie. You look as woeful as a wet washday." Mother told her about my earache and Aunt Carrie said, "It certainly doesn't seem to be troubling her at the moment."

I turned my back and went up to my room without a word. I thought I was noble but Mother scolded me later for being rude. I wish I had dared to tell Mother exactly what I wanted to yell at darling Auntie. But I don't think she knows I know such bad language.

I HATE FOREVER SMILING. My cheeks get exhausted. Then I am tempted to cross my eyes or stick out my tongue. I wonder if that bit about "Lead us not into temptation" in the Lord's Prayer means that kind of temptation. Did kids back then stick out their tongues? I cannot picture Jesus doing it.

It is hard to believe Aunt Carrie is Dad's sister. When she hears me say "Yeah" instead of "Yes" she says I sound like a little Dutch girl. But I have heard her say it herself.

No news about our War Child yet, although some are here in Canada already.

Saturday, June 22, 1940

George was home for a bit because he had to take stuff to the market. He said he wants a boy War Child but he was only teasing. It was nice to see him even though he couldn't stay. He showed off his bulging muscles. They are hard as rocks.

When I want to talk to Mother these days, she is always off at a meeting of the Red Cross or busy knitting socks for the soldiers and busy counting stitches. She is teaching Eleanor to do it too. "Working for The Cause," Aunt Carrie calls it.

I am glad Mother has given up trying to turn me into a knitter. My lost stitches stay lost. So many socks are being sent overseas you would think every soldier was a centipede.

Eleanor keeps turning up the radio so she can listen to Glenn Miller while she knits. Mother groans, but today I saw her toe tapping.

Barbara finally came to supper, but it did not feel like my birthday anymore. Whenever I mention our War Guest, Barbara says I never stop talking about the WG children. I do not understand her. If her family were getting a child, Barbara would talk my ear off about it.

Maybe it is because she will be at camp all summer and she is afraid I won't want to be friends by the time she comes home. Yet we have been friends ever since they moved to Guelph when we were starting Grade Four.

Sunday, June 23, 1940

After church, Aunt Carrie and Grandpa came over. They were all talking about the news. France has surrendered! The Germans are in Paris. Dad said he was not surprised but I don't know why. Aunt Carrie went to Paris once when she was young and she said she could not bear to think of German soldiers "goosestepping through those lovely old streets."

I cannot picture her young. It is almost as impossible as picturing Jesus sticking out his tongue.

I thought of asking Miss Carter about this in Sunday School but she is so proper I couldn't.

Mother and Aunt Carrie have gone to the evening service. I have new library books. I am going to get into bed and read.

Monday, June 24, 1940

Flat feet! That is what the Army won't take. I can't picture them and I can't see why you couldn't march on flat feet. Dad said I soon would if I tried it. He says it would "hurt like billy-oh." Lillian's father picked her up after school to take her to the dentist so I watched him walking, but his feet looked just like everybody else's. I wonder which bit is flat. Maybe the tops of the toes. That wouldn't show in shoes.

Tuesday, June 25, 1940

There was a rainbow in the sky over our house this afternoon and Eleanor and I sang "Somewhere Over the Rainbow" to it.

Do you suppose pilots ever fly through rainbows and forget the War for a minute?

I have a feeling rainbows are too low, but planes have to be low when they are taking off and landing, so it could happen.

Dad says he thinks flying will become a normal way to travel in the next twenty-five years. It does not sound likely to me. They could not take very many people at once, and the planes would be too heavy to get off the ground. Also, I should think lots of people would be too scared of crashing.

Wednesday, June 26, 1940

We had to clean out our desks today. I found a hard old ball of bubble gum stuck in the very back corner of mine. It was furry with dirt. I wanted to leave it there for the next kid to discover, but I didn't.

I said "Ugh!" right out loud and Barbara wanted to know why. I couldn't tell her. Her desk is as clean and neat as a cupboard in a hospital.

I kept the gum in my pocket until we got home and then I put it into a hole in the maple tree out front. I hope no squirrel finds it and thinks it's a nice nut. He'd be as sad as Squirrel Nutkin.

I went to the store with Mother and she bought me an Eskimo Pie. Yum. It is really just an ice cream bar coated with chocolate, nothing to do with any Eskimo and not a pie. I guess they call it that because it is cold.

I told you nothing much happened, Diary. But I did promise Eleanor I would try to write every day.

Thursday, June 27, 1940

School is almost over. No more pencils, no more books, no more teacher's dirty looks. Then the summer will stretch out, full of long sunny days for playing and long rainy hours for reading. Oh, I do hope our WG likes reading! And swimming. And all the other summer things. Strawberries and then raspberries and then blueberries. If only they lasted so you could eat fresh berries all summer and even in the fall. Mother's jam is just not the same. And she won't let us put sugar on our berries. She says they are plenty sweet enough, but they are even better with sugar. There's that sweet scrunch.

It is funny though that they do taste plenty sweet enough when you pick them and pop them straight into your mouth. I love eating fresh berries that way, especially the wild ones.

I have a new autograph book to take to school tomorrow. Mother already wrote in it:

Being a girl is a great adventure.
Being a girl is a wonderful thing.
Something like being a great explorer.
Something like being a king.

I like it even though kings are boys.

Friday, June 28, 1940

School is out at last and I am promoted into Grade Seven. Barbara stood top of the class as usual. She says her mother keeps telling her that all the girls in her family stand top of their class. I'm glad my parents don't expect me to be so brilliant.

The hard thing in Grade Six was decimals and percents. I hope those have been left behind in Grade Seven. And I don't really understand rods and acres. I know miles because it is one mile from our house to Aunt Carrie's. I admit that Math is my least favourite subject. Ever since I skipped Grade Three I have not been fast at multiplying. Mother can do it at the speed of light, but she used to be a teacher before she married Dad. She had to stop then because they don't allow married women to be teachers. I think it is because they believe men are the providers and married women should stay home and not take money from a man with a family to support.

Mother thinks that now so many men are going overseas, the board might have to hire some married women. I wonder if she wishes they would ask her. I can't imagine it. When I come home from school, I like her to be waiting to hear about my day, even when I am not in the mood to say much. Barbara's mother has milk and cookies waiting! But she quizzes Barbara about school while Barbara eats. That would spoil my appetite. My mother just listens.

I am still writing in here because, when Mother called up that I had to turn the light out, I told her I was writing in my diary. She said, "Well, turn it out the moment you finish." So, if I kept writing, I could stay up until dawn.

Saturday, June 29, 1940

Late afternoon

Summer holidays have begun. Hurray!

If only Mother would agree to having summer holidays from housework. There seems to be much more to do when I am not at school. Boring things like dusting and polishing silver and shaking out mops and beating rugs. They aren't big rugs but I still don't like it. Grit blows into your face.

I don't like helping with the washing either. I have to feed the clothes through the wringer into the rinse water and then through again into the basket. I am always nervous because we had a teacher in Grade Two who had a crooked finger from getting it caught in the wringer. Just thinking about it gives me the shivers. Lizby stands on the other side making sure the things land safely in the basket and then we lug them outdoors.

But hanging the clothes out on the line is easier and sometimes even fun if Lizby or Eleanor and I do it together. They are fussy though. If I hang a shirt upside down or something, they make me unpin it and do it their way. I can't see that it matters. Eleanor says I would understand it if I had to do the ironing. I tried to do it once as a grand surprise for them, but I scorched the front of Dad's best shirt. It smelled terrible and a hole was burned right through it. It was mortifying. Mother says she will teach me when I have increased my powers of concentration. Lizby says ironing is no treat and I should put it off as long as possible.

Thank goodness washday only comes once a week. Last Monday I heard Lizby singing "This is the way we wash our clothes." I almost asked her if she learned it at the orphanage, but stopped myself. She sounded so happy.

Stopped to watch a troop of soldiers marching past and singing, "Pack up your troubles in your old kit bag." It made me want to march with them. They sounded so jolly you would think they were off to a giant party. Yet some of them may get wounded or even killed. How can they sound so carefree? I would be scared. Maybe they are but hide it.

Sunday night, June 30, 1940

This afternoon was the Sunday School picnic. I love the squishy tomato sandwiches. Robbie and I went in the egg-and-spoon race and lost. Our side won the tug-of-war though. For a while we were losing but Dad noticed and grabbed hold of the rope and dug in his feet and hauled us to victory.

I wanted to talk to Mother and Dad tonight but they were laughing so hard at "Fibber McGee and Molly" that I couldn't. I don't think it is all that funny. If I let everything come tumbling out of my closet that way, Mother would not smile, let alone laugh out loud. It sounds like an avalanche.

I wish I had a radio all my own in my bedroom instead of having to listen to the big one in the living room. At least we have our old Victrola. When Robbie comes over, he loves winding it up and playing Shirley Temple singing "Animal Crackers in My Soup." I know that he likes playing the other side better though. It goes, "Oh, we wish that we were swallows so we could fly away. That's the song they sing in the singsong in Sing Sing." Sing Sing is a prison.

I wish we had two telephones too. I'm always the one who has to run to answer it when it rings, even though it is usually for one of the others. Barbara's family has one upstairs in case her father gets called by one of his patients during the night. But even she doesn't have her own radio.

JULY

Dominion Day
Monday night, July 1, 1940

Today is Dominion Day, the date that they signed something that joined the provinces and made Canada a country. I don't know if all of them joined. I think some of the western ones came later. Now there are nine and I can recite their names and their capital cities.

Barbara goes to camp tomorrow. I helped her pack some of her stuff. What a long list! It sounds neat. She has to have her own soap dish and her own flashlight and a groundsheet to put over her bedroll when they sleep out. Or under it maybe?

We have heard that our War Guests are on their way. Some have already arrived here in Guelph. My stomach feels queasy when I think about our girl on a ship in the Atlantic with German submarines hiding under the waves. Her parents must be scared to death.

George came home with sparklers for us to light up

because of Dominion Day. But no rockets. The true firecracker day is Queen Victoria's birthday on May 24. But the sparklers are fun as long as you don't hang on too long and crisp your fingertips.

Tuesday, July 2, 1940

Eleanor and her friend Carol and I took sandwiches and hiked out to the Ridge for fun. It was hot and it seemed a long way home. They talked to each other and I wished I had brought a book. But it was better than staying home and doing chores. Eleanor said, "Sitting here in the sunshine with the wind blowing the clouds like that makes it hard to believe we are at war."

I wished she had not reminded us. The clouds were fat and puffy and blew along like clipper ships in full sail. I lay on my back and watched them and loved the whole world. When you look straight up, the very top of the sky is such a deep blue. Not dark. Deep. As though you could swim up into it.

Wednesday, July 3, 1940

Mother came home from grocery shopping today, fuming because people have been saying mean things to the Muellers. Their grandson Albert is in Robbie's class. I never thought about him being German. He's just Albert. I've known them all my life. They came from Germany long ago and have lived in Canada for years. Gus Mueller was in George's class. Anyway, Mother bought some things we didn't even need, to show them she knew they were good people.

Somebody actually threw a rock through their front window. It had a piece of paper tied onto it that said something nasty. And they wrote things on the walls too. Mother would not say what. I feel confused about Germans. They might be spies. But I know that the Muellers would not be spies. They still have accents but they love Canada.

I wonder what a real spy would look like. I guess the Muellers must have relations in Germany still. What if you had relatives who were Nazis? I won't say this to Mother or Dad because I would have to listen to a long lecture about not letting my imagination run away with me.

Will our War Guest girl hate the Nazis? She would have good reason.

Friday, July 5, 1940

Nothing happened yesterday. Well, Mother made me help plant things in the garden. Robbie helped but he got bored and ran off before we were done. Mother says there is still time for lettuces and radishes to grow. I hate radishes.

George is coming home again for the weekend. That means we will have a roast or maybe mock duck.

Mother saves the best food so Georgie can feast. I bet they have great food on his farm – butter and cream and lots of helpings. But I don't mind joining in his feast so I won't say a word.

Saturday, July 6, 1940

I wish George would not tease me as though I were still a little kid. He pulls my hair or grabs me and tickles me sometimes. I HATE being tickled. He also likes snapping dishtowels at me and Eleanor and Lizby. They mostly laugh but it makes me mad. Yet all big brothers seem to do those things. Margaret always used to complain about her brother Ralph being mean and making fun of her.

Now she is living right by the Atlantic Ocean and they can see ships in Halifax harbour. She wrote that they are scared that submarines will come in under water and torpedo them. I asked Dad if it could happen and he started to say not to be so silly, and then he stopped and said he was not sure. It sounds crazy to me.

George is much nicer than Ralph.

Dad found George his job. Farmers need help, with so many men going overseas. I hope George does not think about signing up. He will be old enough in August. I never mention this subject because I know Mother would cry at the very thought. She says she has no favourite child, but Eleanor and I think she has a soft spot for Georgie-porgie.

We went swimming at the quarry today. It was glorious. I can float on my back better than Dad or George. Eleanor mostly sits on the edge and talks with other people her age. She wanted to get a two-piece bathing suit but Mother said she couldn't. As usual, Eleanor gave in without making a fuss. I have a feeling I will make a fuss when I am her age.

I wish Guelph had an outdoor swimming pool like the one in Fergus. We just have that small one in the basement of the YMCA and girls only go when their parents pay for lessons.

Sunday, July 7, 1940

At church this morning, Dr. Gallegher prayed for peace, as usual. Mother says he's helping to plan the War Guests coming to Guelph. I read the Hymnary while he preaches and I memorize my favourites. Some of them are great poems. Like "And did those feet in ancient times." I love learning them so I can say them to myself when I can't sleep.

Lots of the women sit and knit. Mother won't and she won't let Eleanor do it either. You can hear the needles clicking right through the scripture, although they do stop, usually, for the prayers.

I sat and dreamed about the War Child. I wish I knew what she will be like and where she is right now. I hate waiting.

Monday, July 8, 1940

Our War Girl is in Toronto! She has been there for about ten days. We still don't know her name or how old she is. We go to get her on Wednesday! I cannot believe it. What if she is absolutely awful and I have to be nice to her in spite of it? She won't be. But I'll be glad when the waiting is over.

We are going to have to share a room. I will maybe like that sometimes, but I am not sure. I have had a room of my own since I was five. Also I am not a tidy person. What if she is extremely neat? Well, we will just have to work it out.

Tuesday, July 9, 1940

We are going to have TWO children for a while instead of only one. Mr. Bennett was knocked down by a car yesterday and his leg is broken. He is in the hospital. Mrs. Bennett asked if Mother would bring their War Child home with ours and keep him until Mr. Bennett gets back on his feet. Robbie told me. They won't let him in to see his father and he is upset about it. I don't blame him.

So we are going to get both children tomorrow. I keep wondering and wondering what they will be like and all Mother will say is, "Wait and see, Charlotte." I am not a patient person. I wonder why some people are calm like Mother, and others are not a bit calm and are impatient like me. Will I be like Mother when I am a grown-up? It sounds so dull. No valleys or mountain peaks, just flat fields.

Wednesday, July 10, 1940

Sorry my writing is so scrawly. I am in the car on the way to get the WGs. I have you balanced on my knee but you do jiggle and slide.

Dad took the day off. He does not have a class to teach today, which is lucky, but he does see some of his students. He is driving nearly forty miles an hour, way over the speed limit, but Mother has not said a word to slow him down.

We left Guelph early in case we got a flat tire. It sometimes happens just when you have no time to spare. I have my diary with me because I thought we might have to sit and wait and I could tell about what is going on, instead of having to write it all down much later. I am catching on to how to keep a diary. Whenever the car stops for Mother to buy some berries from a roadside booth or for Dad to get gas, I write a couple of sentences.

We have to go to Hart House at the University of Toronto to pick up the children.

My stomach keeps whirling. It also heaves up and down as though I'm on the Tilt-a-whirl ride at the fun fair. But Mother said I could not come along if I was going to get carsick, so I am sucking the barley sugar she keeps in the glove compartment just for me.

Whenever we go to Toronto, we pass through Norval and I always wave to L.M. Montgomery's house. She does not live there now, but maybe her spirit sees me. She is not dead though. Mother knows somebody who used to know her and who has kept in touch. I wanted to see her, but Mother says authors are not sights to be gawked at. They are human beings. I wonder if the WGs know her books.

We'll soon be at Hart House. I can hardly stand the suspense.

Bedtime

They are here! Right this minute, we have two War Guest children in this very house. Their names are Jane and Sam Browning. They are a sister and brother. Jane will be nine in November and Sam turned twelve in January. He is half a year older than I am and half a head shorter!

A lady brought four kids out to meet us, but the tallest one, a boy called Terry, and the smallest, a girl called Trixie or something, weren't ours. They had just come to say goodbye. They had all been on the same ship coming over, and spent time together ever since they left England. Terry was a teenager and not friendly looking. The other one was a really small girl who clutched at Jane and cried. Another lady came and took them away after a few minutes and things got easier.

When I first saw our two, they looked so different from what I had imagined. Sam was dressed in a suit with a jacket and short grey flannel pants. And Jane was wearing a dress with smocking at the neck. It was long and sort of babyish. She had a big bow on top of her head and it was coming loose.

They both looked hot and tired. They also looked sad when they had to say goodbye to those others. I think Jane was scared. She was holding tight to Sam's hand as though she expected he would be torn away any minute.

Jane is sort of chubby and short, with round red cheeks and bright blue eyes. Her hair is light brown and cut in a Dutch bob.

They are so real. That does not say what I feel but, before we met, they were like children in a book. But now they are not like that at all. This will sound peculiar, but they are almost too real. The mystery has gone out of them. They are not exciting or strange like children in a story any longer.

And Jane is so much younger than I am! I am disappointed but I am trying hard not to let it show. It would be terrible for them to come so far and guess that the people who were taking them home were not pleased with them. I am very glad that we did not get Terry, the older boy. He never once smiled.

Sam asked Dad why we drove on the wrong side of the road. I did not know that they did it backwards in England. The driver sits over on the passenger side. Dad said he had driven on the left side in England himself years ago.

"I was lucky not to run over anyone," he said. "I think I came close."

Sam actually grinned for a sec.

Later

After we got home, we were all so hot and tired that Mother sent us to the corner store for popsicles. The WG kids did not say a word until we came out. Then Sam said that they call them "ice lollies." Robbie and I taught them to say popsicles instead so they won't sound peculiar. They remind me of Little Lord Fauntleroy, which is strange since he was an American really.

To get back to my life! I am not sharing a room with Jane yet. This may change later but she burst into tears when Mother told her she would be sleeping in the twin bed in my room and Sam was just across the hall. "I want to stay with Sammy," she blubbered.

Sam looked disgusted but he put his arm around her and asked if she could be in with him on the first night. He is a good brother. Mother said sure and we set up the folding cot in the room where he will be. Jane cheered up then.

Whenever she is not cheered up or gets nervous, she sucks her thumb. I used to do that. Mother reached over and pulled it out of her mouth just the way she used to do with me. She does it gently and she does not say a word, but you stop sucking it until you forget. I remember exactly how it felt. You want to yell that it is YOUR thumb and you should be left to suck it if you like. But you don't dare. Mother says she saved me from having an overbite. That's like buckteeth.

Sam whispered something to Mother and she went and got a rubber sheet. I guess he told her Jane might wet the bed. He looked embarrassed, poor thing.

I used to have to sleep on one of those things. It was stiff and it made noises whenever you turned over. Poor Jane. At least when I used to wet the bed, I was always in my own home and I was younger than nine.

Jane's birthday is on Guy Fawkes' Day. I knew that date was in history but I had to ask Dad what it meant while the WGs were upstairs. Guy Fawkes tried to blow up the British Houses of Parliament with kegs of gunpowder. He got caught and they executed him. British kids still celebrate the day by making a life-sized stuffed "guy" and burning it in a big bonfire. Dad says it is a little like Hallowe'en. When he said that, the WGs looked blank. I did not ask, but I really think they had never heard of Hallowe'en.

Making a Guy sounds a bit weird but maybe we should try it.

Jane calls Sam Sammy but he wants the rest of us to call him Sam. He is very skinny. He has big dark eyes and black hair. It comes right down to his eyebrows. His ears stick out like cup handles. He sounds uppity but I think it is just his accent.

Robbie came over the minute we got home. He took one look at Sammy and said, "Hello, Shrimp!" Jane got red and looked ready to smack Rob, but Sam just grinned and said, "Hello yourself, Infant." I think they will get along fine.

When Sam smiled at Robbie, he looked so different. I guess he was nervous meeting us. Nobody could be nervous meeting Robbie though.

Jane is entirely different. She has freckles and a snub nose and she is very serious most of the time. The only time I saw her smile was when we stopped for ice cream cones in Georgetown. She loves ice cream!!

Nearly midnight

I can't get to sleep so I am going to write a little more and see if that helps. The house is all in darkness and a bit spooky. It is so eerie knowing our two War Guests are just across the hall.

I don't know why their English accents were such a shock to me. I knew they were English the whole time. They keep reminding me of children in British books who have nannies and wear frocks and have tea instead of supper. I almost asked Jane if they had a nanny and then decided not to.

They come from Wembley, which is part of London, I think. Their father has a dairy business with milk wagons pulled by horses. I wonder if they look like our milk wagons.

Sam loves those horses. They aren't riding horses, but he learned to ride them before he could walk. That is what Jane says anyway. Jane doesn't ride them at all because her mother thinks girls have to be ladylike. When she began to talk about her "mum," I thought she would burst out crying. Then Sam said, "Don't forget what Daddy told us." She bit her lip and nodded. When Dad asked what it was, Sam said, "Always remember that we British are the bravest of the brave."

"True enough," Dad said — as though we Canadians were a bunch of cowards. I wanted to say something but did not.

When Jane says my name, it sounds like "Shawlot."

After supper, Aunt Carrie came over with a box of Tinkertoys for Sam. They are nice and he is pleased, I guess, but I think he is a bit too old for them. And what about Jane and me? Why couldn't she give them to all of us?

I just yawned so I will stop writing now.

Thursday, July 11, 1940

Jane did not wet the bed but she screamed with nightmares. I had just fallen asleep when she started. I could hear her clearly, as though she had slept in my room after all. She dreamed they were being bombed or a torpedo hit their ship and she was drowning and she couldn't find Sam. I could hear him calling to her, "I'm right here, Janie. Do hush! I'm right here in the same room." It frightened me so much I had to turn on my light. I fell asleep with it on but Mother came in and turned it out before morning.

They do like reading. They love *The Secret Garden* almost as much as I do. Jane told me that Mary Lennox going to live in England is like them coming here. I wish we really lived in a house like Misselthwaite Manor with a hundred rooms and a secret garden and a robin and a boy like Dickon. I told Jane and she said she does not know anyone who lives in such a place. I thought lots of English people had mansions like that. I know they have castles there. Palaces too. (I don't know the difference.) But Jane says their house is smaller than ours.

It has a name though. Hedges. It seems a queer thing to call a house.

Lizby says lots of British houses have names. We should name our house. But I can't think what would fit. It certainly is not like Misselthwaite Manor and we don't have a hedge.

Friday, July 12, 1940

At breakfast, Dad thumped Sam on the back, rumpled up Jane's hair so her ribbon came undone and kissed me. Then he said, "Don't worry, you three. It'll get easier soon."

I wonder how he knew we were all feeling queer.

Mother asked them what they drank at breakfast at home. Tea! They were surprised when we were surprised. They have cooked food too. Eggs and cooked tomatoes!

This is Orangeman's Day. Tom Reilly, a boy from down the street who is a friend of George's, is in a band and will be marching in the parade. He is a trumpeter. George used to play the trumpet too, but of course he's away and too busy now. I should not be thankful but I am. Trumpet practice is hard to listen to close up. We could hear Tom practising their march on his trumpet.

Later

Mother took us all shopping. The WGs needed some summer clothes. Not dress-up ones — clothes to play in. I had to get a new bathing suit. I wore the seat of mine out sliding on the rocks when we were at the quarry.

We went to The Nuttery with our empty glass jar and the WGs stared as the clerk ground up the peanuts into our container. The oil goes to the top when we get it home but you just stir it in. I love peanut butter. We spread some on bread when we got home but Jane would not even taste it. Sam did, but screwed up his face as though he had been poisoned. He did not spit it out but I could tell that he longed to. I cannot imagine anyone not liking peanut butter. Mother gave them some toast and honey to make up for it.

After the peanut butter, we went to the shoe store and they got to stick their feet into the X-ray machine and see their bones looking all green and ghostly. We kept pushing each other out of the way until the clerk told Mother we would have to leave if we did not "settle down." Mother murmured about Jane and Sam just having come over from England and the clerk changed totally. He smiled and smiled at them and said how nice it was to have them in the store, but I still did not like him. If Mother had not been there, I am sure he would have made us leave.

The British have different words for things. Some of them are strange. Plimsolls are running shoes. Frocks are dresses, of course. I knew that but I would not call mine frocks. Frocks sound fancier than dresses. People say "party frocks." Jumpers are pullovers. Sam scraped his knee and asked for "a plaster." He meant a bandage. They call them "sticking plasters."

Mother says we are lucky to be learning new ways to say old things — like a second language. Jane looked worried. I think she worries a lot. Mother saw that Jane was anxious, I guess, because she explained that we would not have to study our "second language," we would just pick it up as we went along. Jane sighed with relief and said she thought Mother meant she would have to learn French. Somebody had told them all Canadians speak French. I laughed but Mother explained that most English-speaking Canadians study French in high school.

"I wish I could speak French," she went on, "but I can't. I only remember a few words and phrases. They should start children learning French when they are much younger. It is so much easier for small children to pick up a language."

Jane asked how young and Mother laughed and said she need not worry because it wouldn't happen until she was too old. Jane was relieved and so was I.

When the shopping was done, we went to the park and played on the swings. Jane did not want to come home even for lunch.

Then, halfway home, we realized she was not with us. When we turned to look for her she was half a block behind us, sitting on the sidewalk and playing with a Scottie puppy a woman had out for a walk.

Sam told us very fast that they had had to leave their dog with their grandparents in Coventry. They gave Jane the puppy for her birthday a year ago, before they knew she would have to come to Canada. They said they would keep him for her until she comes back. Jane misses him a lot. He is a Scottie called Skipper. Sure enough, when Jane came running to catch up, she was rubbing away tears. Nobody said a word, but Mother held her hand the rest of the way.

I have decided to make lists of all the words we use differently. I won't do it all at once but will add more as I learn them. Some I already know, of course, from reading British books.

I'll get Jane to tell me any she notices. She has already told me a couple.

British words/Canadian words

frock: dress
jumper: pullover sweater
plaster: bandage (it is short for "sticking plaster")
ice lolly: popsicle
vest: undershirt

There, that's a start.

After supper

An airplane flew over this morning when we were on our way home from the park, and Sam and Jane stopped dead and stared up at it.

Then she said, "Is it one of ours?"

"Of course," Sam said. "No enemy planes would fly over Canada, Goosie."

The very idea of German planes ever flying over Guelph shocked me so that I could not think of anything to say. I've heard of people having water on the brain. I felt as though I had ice water on the knees for a few seconds. Everything about the War has always seemed so far away and unreal. But it has not been that way for Jane and Sam. And they have brought the horror of it with them. They have gas masks and, at school, they had air-raid drills, practice ones, so they would know what to do if the bombing started.

When I noticed planes before, I was interested, never afraid. Now they are menacing even though I know we don't have any bombers flying over.

Strangest of all is how I shiver and, a few minutes later, I have forgotten the War is still going on. When I remember, it makes me feel heartless. I wonder if the Brownings forget. I think they must, but not as quickly as I do. I'll bet Jane is forever wondering about her dog.

Bedtime

A few minutes ago, when Dad said we must turn off the radio and get to bed, Jane said, "But not the lights. In Canada, you leave on the lights. It was so lovely when we first saw. We could scarcely believe it."

We stared at her until Sam told us how amazed they were when they got to Canada and night came and there was no blackout. Where they live, if there isn't a moon, you can't see anything because there is no light showing from any windows, and no street lights either. If you absolutely have to go out, you carry a "torch." That was what Jane said and I thought, at first, she meant a fiery torch like the ones they have in books, but she meant a flashlight. You put your hand half over the beam to keep it from showing and, if planes should come, you turn it off fast.

"What if there's a moon?" I asked.

"My father calls a full moon a bomber's moon," Sam said in a low voice and Jane shuddered.

"The moonlight might help them see where to drop their bombs," Sam went on, as if I had not enough sense to figure that out for myself.

I love looking at the full moon and it is always in love songs and poems. It is sad to think of people being afraid of its light.

Jane asked me where my grandparents lived. Her father's parents are dead and her mother's are the ones who live in Coventry. They are the ones looking after Jane's dog. That is where their mother was brought up. I explained that Mother's mother died when I was six and her father died before I was even born. Grandma Twiss died last summer and now Grandpa lives with Aunt Carrie. Poor old Grandpa!

"My grandpa is my best friend," Jane told me very seriously. "He gave me Skip, you know. We visit in the holidays. He must be missing me a lot." Then she said,

"He promised to keep petting Skip for me. And he said he would write and tell me about how Skip is. But he hasn't done it."

Her voice shook. I thought she would burst into tears.

I said there has not been time for a letter to get to us yet. She said she would write to him tonight and she cheered up.

Saturday, July 13, 1940

After supper

At breakfast, Sam asked Jane if she had noticed the French on the money and Jane pointed out that she has no money.

"Saturday is our day for giving out allowances," Dad said, quick as a wink. "I'll make sure you get money with French on it." He was partly joking, of course. All our money has French on it. Jane was so pleased. Sam looked a bit worried until Dad said he'd had the allowance ready to give them all along. And I said it really was allowance day.

Their money has all different words too but you can't put them side by side because it is too different. We have dimes and nickels and quarters and they have shillings and pence and pounds but nothing comes out the same. Sam thinks a shilling is about twenty cents but he didn't seem sure. I like the words like "tuppence" and "ha'penny." They sound like words in a book.

Now Mother and the WGs are sorting through their belongings and I actually feel like writing in you, dear Diary, while I am by myself. One of the good things about a diary is that you can write down your innermost feelings, even the ones you are ashamed of, and nobody will know. I am supposed to like the WGs and I mostly do, Diary, but every so often I wish they had not come. The house feels crowded and you never have a chance to talk just to Mother without somebody else listening or butting in. She seems busy with them all the time too. They aren't babies, but she treats them as if they are.

Eleanor also pays far more attention to them than she does to her own sister. I guess she is trying to make them feel at home, but she goes overboard.

Sometimes I feel invisible, Diary. Dad is up at the college so much that I have hardly any time alone with him either. He has extra work with all his projects at the experimental farm, because so many students have enlisted. He is a soil scientist. I don't know exactly what he does but I've heard Mother telling him he must get more help. He does seem to be home a bit more since the WGs came though. I wonder if it is because Sam is a boy and Dad thinks he needs a man to take his father's place or something. I know Dad misses George.

Jane has not moved in with me yet, but I think she will soon. Sam spends time riding George's old bike around the neighbourhood, although he has to concentrate on not riding on the right side of the road. That is funny. I just realized that in his mind, on the road, right is wrong.

I took Jane and Sam to the library this morning and got them library cards. When Miss Walters told them they could get out two blue-card books or one blue-card and one white-card, they could not understand why. White cards are the fiction ones. I get three because I have borrowed George and Eleanor's cards. I don't like the blue-card ones. They are full of facts — history and science and stuff. Jane did not want blue cards either, but Sam said some were good and he found one about airplanes and one about dogs. Jane and I got four Oz books. I am reading my way through them all in order.

When they had to sign their names in the book, Jane dipped the pen nib in the ink perfectly but didn't let the extra ink drip before she tried to write with it. She stared at the blot she'd made and went red as fire. She nearly cried but Miss Walters turned the pages back and showed her that lots of other children had done the same thing. I think maybe I did, but I kept quiet about it.

We all joined the Summer Reading Club. There's going to be a prize for the child who reads the most books. You could win it easily if you just read all the skinny ones, but I like thick ones better. I wish the prize was a book.

Just before supper, Dad put on the hose and we got into our bathing suits and ran through the water. Robbie came over and then John from farther up the street and the twins Elsie and Norma — they are younger than Jane, but they are a bit prissy. They screech and flap their hands whenever the spray gets close to them. Their mother calls them home when she hears them squealing.

I am doing my best to enjoy having Sam and Jane here even though I do wish Jane was older. I think they are homesick, but they don't say so. Maybe they forget, when things are happening. Maybe they are doing their best to enjoy being here even though it is not easy for them either. Maybe they are hiding innermost feelings too.

I do wish people would stop forever asking them how their family is and how they are liking Canada. It happens wherever we go. Jane and Sam are always polite, but it is tough because it just reminds them of their families and then they get lonelier.

Today the kids told us they were surprised not to see Mounties riding around everywhere. They thought Mounties were the regular policemen in Canada. Jane said she was looking forward to maybe even speaking to one. I felt we had let them down, but it was funny too. I've hardly ever seen one myself. I think they work more out west and in the North West Territories. But I am not sure.

Sunday, July 14, 1940

I had to stand up in Sunday School this afternoon and introduce Jane and Sam. It should have been a snap but it wasn't. My face went red as a beet. So did Sam's. Jane beamed at everyone.

After supper

Aunt Carrie came for tea and told us about a soldier bringing a bird to the canteen where she was passing out sandwiches. He had bought it because he was lonely, but now he is shipping out and the Army says he cannot keep it. They told him to wring its neck or let it go free, but he couldn't.

"What did he do with it?" Jane asked, looking very anxious.

Aunt Carrie stared out the window and muttered, "He gave it to me. I was going to bring it to you, but Father took a fancy to it so we are keeping it. Its name is Winnie."

We could not believe our ears.

After supper, we went over to see Winnie. He is named after Winston Churchill. He is very cute. He looked at Mother and said, "Hubba, hubba." That was the first time I heard Jane really laugh.

Monday, July 15, 1940

Dad took Sam to the barbershop today because his hair is growing right down into his eyes. We expected him to come home with short hair, maybe even a brush cut like the soldiers. But it was only trimmed about half an inch. When the barber asked him how short he wanted it, Sam said they mustn't make it too short or his mother would not know him. Dad promised to take a picture for him to send to England. Mother has trimmed Jane's bangs and Dad went out to get a new film so he can take pictures of both of them and of us and our house so they could mail them home.

"We should get two sets in case of torpedoes," Sam said.

There was a funny silence and then Dad said he would be sure to take two sets and send them on separate days to be certain they would reach England safely.

Then, all of a sudden, Jane started telling us about lifeboat drills. She talked faster and faster and finally Mother pulled her onto her lap and said, "Easy does it, Janie. It's over now." And when Jane started sucking her thumb, Mother did not pull it out of her mouth.

Then Dad came back and began to snap away with his Brownie camera and Jane stopped looking queer. He used up two whole films and went right down to the drugstore to get the developing started. The pictures should be ready next week.

Mother produced a surprise for Sam and Jane. She had found a jar of something called Marmite to spread on their bread instead of peanut butter. They smiled and smiled. They made me try it. Diary, I think it tastes disgusting. Well, maybe not quite that bad, but definitely strange. It has a horrid smell. I said I did not see why the kids thought it was good.

"It tastes like home to you, doesn't it, Jane?" Mother said, smiling at my expression.

What would taste like home to me if I were sent to England? Corn on the cob? We had it last night for supper and the WGs had never had it before. Can you believe that, dear Diary? They had never once eaten a cob of corn. They call it maize and feed it to animals. They liked it though, once they got over being surprised.

Maybe johnnycake with maple syrup is a taste of home for me. They don't have maple syrup in England. They have treacle and something called "golden syrup." Treacle is a strange word. It sounds as though it trickles but Jane says not.

Tuesday, July 16, 1940

Jane's bedtime

Today Jane moved her things into my room. Now she is in the other twin bed. I came to bed early to keep her company on this first night away from Sam. She looks small and as if she is trying not to cry. I don't know what to do. She is staring at me while I write this. I am sure she feels terribly homesick, but I can't think how to help!

Later

I was inspired all at once. I got up and got my music box. It is very nice to listen to while you are going to sleep. It plays "Lullaby and Good Night" over and over until it winds down.

It is working! Jane is smiling, though she still looks a bit misty. I'll turn out the light and we can both listen. The hall light is shining through the open door. That'll help.

Wednesday, July 17, 1940

In the middle of the night Jane had a bad dream and wanted Sam, but after he came, she had a drink of milk and asked me to turn on the music again and she stayed. She is brave. Well, I knew that, of course. As their father said, the bravest of the brave! But she must long for her mother to come to her instead of mine. I have seen her mother's picture. She is shorter than Mother and much fatter, with glasses and curly hair. I bet she gives good hugs, sort of warm and squishy.

I would like Mother's better, even if you can

feel her bones. I can remember sitting on her lap though and she did not feel too boney then. Far nicer than Aunt Carrie, who is fat.

Just a month ago today it was my birthday and Mother told us about the War Guests coming, and now it seems as though they have been here forever.

Mother and Dad are talking about all of us going away for a week's holiday in Muskoka. I have been to Muskoka before. It was great. I was telling Jane and she said, "Is it like the seashore or the Lake District?" I guess the right answer is the place with lakes. There is no sea in Ontario. But maybe Lake Ontario and Lake Huron look like oceans. You can't see across to the other side. But the waves are not so big and they are not salty.

Dad and Sam keep discussing the fighter planes and the likelihood of bombing. I guess Dad is trying to be truthful about what is happening, but I hate hearing about it. They train some of the pilots here in Canada. I hope George does not get caught up in it and decide he has to join up. I think it might kill Mother.

I wonder if she thinks about this. She must. But she does not speak a word about it.

Thursday night, July 18, 1940

We are going to a lodge on Three Mile Lake. Dad chose it because we sleep in a cabin there but eat in the main lodge and Mother will not have to cook. Lizby is going to Aunt Carrie's.

I go around singing, "Blue lake and rocky shore, I will return once more." Jane sings along. She says they sang it at her cousin's Girl Guide camp. She says her cousin knows all our songs. Sam won't sing a note.

"Father hardly ever sings either," Jane told me. Then she looked away and muttered, "Except for just before we left. He kept singing 'Rule Britannia' and 'Bless 'Em All.'"

I did not know what to say so I kept quiet. My father sings a lot, especially in the shower or when we are all going somewhere in the car. He likes making fun of songs that are supposed to be serious, like "Annie Laurie."

Friday night, July 19, 1940

I got a postcard from Barbara with a picture of the lodge at her camp on it. It is big and made of logs. It says, *Dear Charlotte, I am having fun. Hope you are too. Love, Barbara Steiner.*

As if I wouldn't know who "Barbara" was!

I was going to write back to her, and Mother suggested I send her a parcel instead. She said getting mail at camp is important. She was already packing up a box to send to the Brownings, so she helped me. Jane watched and made comments. I sent Barbara a new movie magazine, two packages of Lifesavers, some toffee and a little horoscope book so she can tell fortunes. Mother had meant to give it to me on my birthday, but forgot. The box for the Brownings was much heavier. It had a tinned ham in it and cheese and homemade candy and some maple sugar to show it is from Canada. Both the WGs were pleased.

Soon we will have the pictures Dad took and we'll send those too.

I think Barbara will be pleased and very surprised!

We had fresh berries for supper and Sam asked for clotted cream. It sounds horrible to me, but Jane licked her lips at the very thought. Mother said she could whip some cream, but it would not be the same.

It was so hot that Dad turned on the hose for us after supper again. Eleanor started by saying she was too old, but Jane coaxed her until she gave in. You should have heard her screech, dear Diary. You would never think she is almost an adult.

Some more British expressions

torch: flashlight
treacle: syrup
maize: corn
Marmite: no word for it
clotted cream: certainly not like whipped cream
(another British food that sounds awful although
Mother says I would love it)

Saturday night, July 20, 1940

Today the bunch of us got playing that we were putting on a circus. Then the boys ran away and we could not go on with it. They were horrible. Jane was even mad at Saint Samuel.

Then Jane and I made lemonade to sell. We earned nearly three dollars. Dad bought three glasses and told us to keep the change. That helped. We are donating the money to the Humane Society. They rescue stray dogs and cats. This was Jane's idea.

We are going to Muskoka first thing Monday morning and coming back next weekend. Robbie wanted to come too, but there won't be room for him in the car. When Mother told him he would have to sit on Eleanor's knee all the way, he stopped begging. He looked horrified. Eleanor looked a bit horrified too.

We were all sitting out on the Bennetts' front verandah. Robbie's father is home now, with his leg in a plaster cast. He uses crutches and keeps his weight off his bad leg.

"It's about time you had a young man on your knee, Eleanor," he said, teasing her.

"Never," Eleanor said.

"The girl sits on the *boy's* knee," Jane said very seriously.

Even Eleanor laughed. When we get home from Muskoka, Sam will be moving in with the Bennetts.

Nobody mentions this because of Jane. But she has had no nightmare for two nights.

I can hardly wait till it is time to go to the lake.

Sunday, July 21, 1940

This morning Jane dropped her collection in church. Mother had tied it into the corner of a hand-kerchief, but Jane undid it during the Long Prayer. It rolled under the pew and rang when it fell over. She went red as fire. A minute later Sam dropped his and then, doing my best to help, I dropped mine. I knew better but I couldn't resist. Jane looked so miserable. Besides, it was fun.

I almost went into a fit of giggles until Dad gave me a look that stopped them cold. Eleanor laughed and laughed. She was sitting in the choir stall where she could look down at the congregation, all those fancy hats whispering to each other in bobbing bunches. She says Robbie started to put his hand into his pocket too, but his mother glared at him and he pulled his hand back out fast.

Monday, July 22, 1940

Inverness Lodge

Dad picked up the pictures right after breakfast. They were great. We mailed them off to England on the way out of town.

We were so crowded in the car you could hardly breathe. Jane was between Mother and Dad in the front but she spent most of the time on Mother's lap. Sam was in the back with me and Eleanor. We had baskets of food and boxes of toys and books and big thermos jugs of water too. For the first time in my life, I was glad we had no dog.

We stopped by to say goodbye to Grandpa. He was on the porch with Winnie in his cage. Grandpa tried to get the bird to say "Bye-bye" but all Winnie would say was "Bi, toots."

We sang car songs and played Eye Spy and Twenty Questions, but it still took years to get here. Mother twisted around and read to us. We are reading *The Five Children and It*. It is good. Even Eleanor likes it. Those children make such good wishes and then they go so incredibly wrong. We have all tried to figure out a perfect wish. So far, we have not found one that was exciting and foolproof both. I thought of wishing I was a boy for one year, but what if I got stuck and ended up turning into a man. I am sure I would hate it. Their clothes are so dull, for one thing.

Jane decided she would wish for a pet monkey, but Dad said you can't housebreak them. Thoughts of Jane changing her monkey's diapers got us laughing so hard we gave up wishing.

It is lovely here. We live in cabins but we all go in to the big dining room for meals. We swim every day, as much as we can. We always have to have an adult watching. Thank goodness Eleanor counts as an adult! She remembers how hard it is when nobody will lifeguard.

I am learning the flutter kick. You do it with the Australian crawl. You have to keep your knees stiff. And roll your head sideways to breathe. It is hard but it is really fast. Sam does it perfectly. He says he learned it at school in the bathing pool. I wish we had a pool at school.

We brought a croquet set and there is a big flat green space perfect for playing. Sam is good at it and so is Eleanor but I am not. I still like trying. Mother called me a good sport, which was nice.

After supper tonight, we went for a walk and met a skunk strolling along as though he owned the world. We started to run and then saw Sam and Jane were just standing smiling at him. I dragged Jane away and Sam caught on and ran too, but when we were out of spray range, they told us they had never seen a skunk before. They don't have them in England. I could hardly believe it.

The skunk sprayed one of the dogs belonging to the lodge later in the evening. Poor thing. It whimpered and kept pawing at its face. Mr. Sutton, who runs the lodge, gave it a bath in tomato juice, but it still smells pretty bad. And it keeps rubbing its face in the grass as though its eyes sting.

Wednesday, July 24, 1940

Today was absolutely horrible. Mr. Sutton came and told Dad that the skunk had gotten in under one of the cabins and he planned to shoot it. Would Dad come and help out? I was sure Dad would say no, but he went and so did Sam. I cried and so did Jane and Eleanor, but the men paid no attention. Sam looked pretty sick. They managed to kill it and then Jane asked if it might have babies somewhere, which started us crying again.

I asked Sam what it felt like and he said he hated it until he told himself the skunk was Hitler. But it didn't help. He confessed to me later, in secret, that he threw up behind the cabin after it was over.

I woke up hating Dad. He has changed into somebody else today. He seems cold and heartless. I think that I cannot forgive him. But you can't go on hating your father. Not if you really love him.

The holiday felt completely ruined and then George phoned to say he was coming to see us. He's hitch-hiking. Mother worries, but not enough to tell him to stay at the farm.

Thursday, July 25, 1940

Don't feel like writing. Maybe I'll give up keeping a diary. I just bet George doesn't come.

Friday, July 26, 1940

It is dark in this cabin at night. I still feel dark inside once the sun sets. But I have to get over it. This is our holiday. Shooting that skunk was not Dad's idea. Mother told me, when we were alone for a minute, that Dad hated it too. She said, "Charles told me that he felt sick, especially when Jane asked if the skunk might have had babies." It turned out it could not because it was a male skunk. At least Mother made me feel better about Dad.

In some way, this seems connected up with the War, but I can't think it through — except I wonder if lots of young soldiers feel like Sam when they have to shoot the enemy. Maybe that is crazy. Would dropping bombs be easier or harder?

George should be here any time now.

Did I ever tell you, Diary, that I am named Charlotte after Dad, who is Charles, and Eleanor is named for Mother, whose name is Ellen? I asked who George was named after and Mother finally admitted they named him after the king because he was a prince of a baby. She was smiling when she said it so she might have been joking.

Saturday, July 27, 1940

George did come, but not until I had been sent to bed. It is great having him with us. He's another adult to watch us swim, for one thing. He does not seem as old as he is, although he is very brown from being out in the sun and he has gigantic muscles now. He keeps getting us to squeeze his arm or punch his middle. Sam is truly impressed.

We went canoeing today and I learned how to paddle in the bow. It was absolutely marvellous. We slid through the water without any noise. Well, only a little. My unhappiness slipped away like the water drops off my paddle. Dad taught me how to stroke to a song, "Swing low, sweet chariot." It was magical.

Sam and George had their own canoe. Jane would not come because it was too tippy. Sam loved it though, just like me. I wonder if we will get good enough to go out on our own after George leaves. He has to get back to the farm tomorrow. I am going to miss him a lot. Today we played Kick the Can and I ran so fast I tripped and fell flat. George helped me up and did not laugh.

Monday, July 29, 1940

We saw falling stars tonight and fireflies. It was lovely. Everyone made wishes. I guess I should have wished the War would end, but I wished we could go out in the canoe again. And we are going to do it. So maybe wishes actually work. If there is a falling star to help! Sam told us that when they were at sea, on the way to

Canada, they saw the Northern Lights. I've never seen them but Dad has. Jane said they were... Then she was stuck for a word. And Sam said, "Enchanting." It sounded perfect.

Tuesday, July 30, 1940

We went out in the canoe twice. The second time was just as it was getting dark. We sang while we paddled and it was such fun. Dad said we could stay out later because it was such a beautiful night with the moon shining on the water. I guess it was what Sam called "a bomber's moon" but here in Muskoka it was simply splendid. There were people at the other end of the lake singing "Alouette" around a campfire. When they got to the chorus, we sang back from our canoe. They stopped dead and then started up again and we sang back and forth all the way to the end without stopping. It is such a happy song, which is surprising when it is all about plucking out a bird's feathers.

I am going to put you away until we get home, Diary. I almost dropped you in the lake when we were down on the dock and it is hard to concentrate here. On writing, I mean.

AUGUST

Friday, August 2, 1940

When we got home, we found mail from England waiting. At last! The people in Toronto sent the letters on. I think their parents must have written almost as soon as Jane and Sam left. They were laughing when they read the letters and crying after they finished. Well, Jane cried. Sam managed not to by sniffing and staring into space. The parcel we sent over to the Brownings had not arrived when they wrote, of course. Mail coming for the WGs seems both wonderful and hard. I can see that it will always remind Jane and Sam of home. They long for news but the letters will make them feel even lonelier.

Lizby welcomed us home by making johnnycake for dessert. Yummy.

Nobody said a word about Sam moving to the Bennetts' tomorrow. I wonder if Jane has forgotten or if she is just pretending or if she maybe does not mind. I cannot tell. She is curled up in a ball in the other bed and she is sucking her thumb and listening to the music box for the umpteenth time. I guess she remembers but cannot talk about it. Poor old Janie!

I got another card from Barbara, by the way. She loved the parcel!

Saturday, August 3, 1940

Sam went over to the Bennetts' this afternoon, but it was okay because we all went too. They have set up a ping-pong table on their back verandah and we took turns playing, even Jane.

She was half asleep in their hammock when it was time to come home. Dad carried her and put her into bed with her clothes still on. Mother came up after a while and sort of slid her out of her dress and into her nightgown. Luckily she was barefoot. Maybe everything will be fine.

Maybe Sam is the homesick one. I looked back and he was staying behind, staring after us. He looked so alone standing there all by himself. I thought boys were supposed to be tough, but I turned around and waved until he waved back.

"See you tomorrow," I called, but softly so Jane would not hear.

When we came in, Dad said he will get out the tent and we kids can sleep out in it some night. Luckily it is a large tent with plenty of room for all of us.

Sunday, August 4, 1940

Church this morning. Sunday School this afternoon. Read my library book this afternoon too. It is an old book called *Prudence of the Parsonage*. It is a bit soppy. Prudence says she will not kiss a boy because she is saving her lips for her future husband. I had to laugh. George was home for the day and he wanted to know what was so funny. I read it to him and he said solemnly, "Charlotte, why are you laughing? That Prudence is a girl after my own heart."

I went to the evening service with Mother. We sang "Day is Dying in the West" and "Abide with me." I like the evening hymns. Too bad we don't sing them in the morning.

Now we are in bed and today is finished. I feel extra tired. Jane is asleep already. And the sun has not quite done setting. Good night.

Monday, August 5, 1940

You will not believe this, Diary, but we woke up this morning covered with speckles. Even Eleanor had spots. The doctor took one look and told us we have German measles! We won't call them that, whatever he says. We feel quite fine really and only mind having to stay home. That must have been what made me feel so tired last night. We felt better when we found out that Sam has them too. That kid up at Inverness who was always whining must have given them to us.

Mother offered to have Sam move back in with us but Robbie's mother says he had the measles when he was a toddler, so he won't catch them now. Why couldn't the measles have come during school?

We played Monopoly all afternoon. Sam won but I might have if I hadn't been helping Jane and Robbie.

Maybe I shouldn't write in you, dear Diary, until the speckles fade away. They make a good excuse for taking a rest from keeping a journal. Yet I think I might miss telling you things. You aren't as troublesome as I thought you would be. See you later, Diary.

Sunday, August 11, 1940

Our spots are practically all gone so Mother made us go to church. We were ordered not to mention them. But everybody knew because Robbie had spread the word around. Nobody sat too close to us.

The scripture was about Jesus healing a sick little girl. Jane whispered to me, "Do you think she might have had German measles?" I did not think so. I don't remember the Bible mentioning Germans or any other country we have now. Yet Germany must have been there. Maybe they never went that far. You wouldn't if you had to walk.

I wish we could play Monopoly but Mother says it is not a Sunday game. All that money makes it evil, I suppose.

I taught Jane to make hollyhock dolls for a while and then we went to our room and played Fish. Jane loves it, which I would think was strange except I loved it myself when I was her age. It would be deadly dull now, except that she gets so excited and her face positively glows when she wins.

Monday, August 12, 1940

Our spots are completely gone and we never really felt sick. Even if they are German, they are the best kind of measles to have. You feel MUCH worse with Red Measles.

We are going to the motion pictures this afternoon. I hope Jane and Sam won't be upset by the newsreels. Last time they showed Hitler himself. He looked like a crazy puppet, waving his arms and screeching. Some of the big kids began to yell, "Heil, Hitler!" and laughed, but the usher told them to stop. They didn't until the cartoons started.

The newsreel showed some of the sailboats that made it over and back at Dunkirk. On the way home, Sam said they brought more than 300,000 of our soldiers across the Channel, with hundreds of small ships helping the Navy. I asked how small and he said there were all sizes but some only had room for two or three men. Those went back over and over. I knew this but I did not say so.

I am really writing a lot in this diary. I am surprised by this, since I was sure I would not. And it isn't just to get that prize Eleanor promised me either.

I guess I have discovered that my life is like a story

and I want to catch it before it gets away. I used to believe I could remember everything that mattered about myself, even the small details, but I know now that this is not true. Already I have forgotten whole days and weeks. It is almost as though I didn't live the first three years, for instance. My earliest memory is of falling downstairs when I was four. I cut my head open on the newel post and there was blood everywhere. I can still see the scene and I still have the scar. But I don't remember what happened next. It is a total blank. So you are important, dear Diary, for you will not let my life get lost.

Bedtime

Tonight Jane was writing a letter home. I wonder what she writes about us. If she kept a diary, what would it say?

My idea of an excerpt from Jane Browning's diary

We are safe in Canada and living with the Twiss family. Charlotte is the nicest girl I have ever met. She took us to a movie show. She keeps me from being too homesick. This is an absolutely wonderful family.

I am doing my best to be nice to her, even though I wish she was older. I think she and Sam are still homesick, but they don't say so. Maybe they forget about home a little when things are happening.

Tuesday, August 13, 1940

When Jane and Sam first came, Sam told us he does not sing. But today Jane told me, in secret, that he is in the choir at home. He just does not want to be a choirboy in Canada. We'll see. We don't have a children's choir every Sunday at our church but we always do around Christmas and Easter. Miss Little leads us and she can get kids to come even when they do not really want to. I like it. Maybe she'll talk Sam around.

Wednesday, August 14, 1940

Today Mother and the WGs and I were downtown and ran into the little girl we met when we picked up Sam and Jane at Hart House. They call her Pixie although her name is really Penelope Buckingham. She was across the street and I would not have known her, but she saw Sam and Jane and let out a scream of joy. She started bouncing up and down in a five-year-old jubilation. (That is what Mother called it.)

Jane knew her at once and began dancing up and down too. A big woman, who looked tired and very grumpy, had hold of Pixie's hand and she gave it a jerk that made her stagger. All the dance went out of her. It was horrible. The woman glanced over at us and her face looked hard as cement. She began to drag Pixie away but Sam ran after them and caught her arm. Then he talked fast. We could hear him explaining that they knew Pixie because they had come to Canada on the same ship and been together in Toronto. The woman, who is Pixie's aunt, stopped scowling but she said they could not stop to talk right now. Her twins were at home alone and who knew what trouble they would be getting into. (We only heard half of this but Sam filled us in later.) He stuck to his guns though, and only let the woman go when he had found out where Pixie is living. It is easy to remember because it is on London Road.

"Pixie's only five and she kept crying almost the whole trip over from England," Sam said. He sounded sad himself when he told us this part.

"Poor little soul," Mother said.

Sam and Jane told us they had heard Pixie was going to stay with her uncle and aunt. But how could her own aunt be so mean? The Brownings want to go and make sure she is all right. Jane says Pixie needs taking care of.

I tried to remember exactly how she had looked that day in Toronto, but I couldn't. Her aunt did seem cross, but Aunt Carrie can be a real grouch when she is tired, so I am not sure Pixie's aunt is all bad.

"Since we know where to find her, let's go home and make a plan," Mother said. "I promise we'll do our best to find out what the problem is."

But when we got home, Dad said we should leave it to the authorities. I could not believe he would be so cold-hearted. It was like the night they shot the skunk.

But he did not see Pixie. It was awful. She was so small and her aunt was so large. Not just large. Hard — like a big boulder.

Mother said, in her frostiest voice, "Charles, it was clear the child was wretched, but we can wait a day or two, if you do not trust our judgment."

She turned her back and went to the kitchen. I think she made Dad think twice. At supper, we ate mostly in silence. Nobody enjoyed the shepherd's pie except me. I love shepherd's pie. Then Dad had to go to a meeting and nothing else happened. Tomorrow though, the others and I will talk by ourselves and see if we can think of a way to rescue Pixie.

After we came up to bed, Jane still went on and on about her. I felt sorry for the kid, but I wish Jane would stop harping on how sad she looked and how awful her aunt was. I want to forget her for a while and go on reading my Oz book. Maybe I am a hard-hearted person. Being soft-hearted all the time wears you out though.

Thursday, August 15, 1940

Today was George's eighteenth birthday but he was not home. Mother had sent a box of cookies home with him to be opened this morning. Sam and I sneaked a couple out of the box. They were yummy. She saves up everything special for her darling George. I think

Mother still sees him as her little boy even though he is practically a man.

Today Pixie was the centre of attention though.

At breakfast, before we had a chance to talk on our own, Mother said she would go with us to Pixie's. She had found some little girl clothes which had been donated to the church clothing drive and some old toys and books of mine to give them. The family doesn't live so very far away from us, so we could go this afternoon. Dad just sat behind the newspaper and did not say one word. I almost said I refused to give away a couple of the books. One was the story of Ferdinand and another was *The Tale of Peter Rabbit*. I really love them and they are mine. My name is written in them and I think we should keep them and give Pixie other ones. But I did not say so. I did not want Sam and Jane to think I was a pig.

I never put down what Pixie looks like. She is tiny. She looks as though she is three or four. Her hair hangs down her back in two long, skinny pigtails. It looks dirty. Her braids remind me of the ball of string Mother and Lizby collected ages ago before we got a big new ball. The old one is fuzzy and brownish and nobody uses it. The ends of Pixie's braids were tied with that sort of string.

Jane says Pixie's eyes are the same grey as rain clouds. She made them sound like the eyes in the Anne books.

Sam thinks she comes from Liverpool. He does not know what her father does but Pixie said something about him driving a lorry. (A lorry is a truck. It will go in my next list.)

I wish the time would pass faster, but Grandpa Twiss says I should not wish my life away. Back to Oz until after lunch.

Bedtime

We went. Jane got Pixie to come out to play while Mother took in the things she had brought to give to Pixie's aunt, Mrs. Buckingham. I wanted to hear what the adults said, so I slid in at Mother's back. Mother made a speech about having two War Guest children and knowing how it could mean a lot of extra expense, so she had brought over some things Pixie might be able to use. The woman was cross at first but then she saw the dresses and other pretty things and started going through them, holding them up one by one. She warmed up as she saw how nice some of them were.

Then she told Mother all about how they had been sent Penelope.

Pixie's dad and Mr. Buckingham are stepbrothers, but the brother in Canada is a lot older and they have never been close. When Mr. and Mrs. B were married, ages ago, the two of them went to England so she could meet his family and see where he had been brought up.

At the time, the men said they must keep in touch. "When war was declared," Pixie's aunt told Mother, "Herbert wrote to say 'Let us know if there is anything we can do for you.'"

"That was generous," my mother said.

"Yes," Mrs. B said. "But he was not prepared for what happened. All at once, when it looked like England could be invaded, Penelope's father just wrote us that she was coming and shipped her out. She was already at sea by the time we got his letter. Pixie's brother stayed behind since he's big enough to work."

"Heavens!" my mother said.

"My Herbert had forgotten about that promise of his, so you can imagine how stunned we were when we were told that 'our' little girl had arrived from England."

After all, she said, their twins were much older and used up all her energy. (Seems she was forty when they were born. I did not think people that old had babies.)

She went on and on. Her husband expects her to do EVERYTHING for Pixie, who isn't old enough to be left on her own. And she wets her bed.

Imagine, dear Diary, how it must feel to be Pixie and to know nobody wants you. I felt a little sorry for her aunt, but none of it is Pixie's fault. We left at last. Mother asked if Pixie could come over to visit us and Mrs. B jumped at it. So Pixie is coming here tomorrow, and on the weekend too.

But she will have to go back there, of course. Poor kid.

Happy birthday, George. Good night, Diary.

Friday, August 16, 1940

Pixie came today. Mrs. B brought her right at noon. Mother waved goodbye to the old bat. Then she took poor Pixie upstairs and washed her from top to toe. Pixie squeaked a bit, but that was all. Mother brushed out her hair and tied a blue ribbon around it. She looked like Alice in Wonderland. I guess the greyness was mostly dirt, I think. Dirt and despair. Then Mother gave her a big glass of milk and toast spread with Marmite. I tried not to stare but I never saw anyone gobble food so fast.

Then, at last, we went out to play. She was so quiet at first she reminded me of a mouse. When it began to rain, we went to the library. Pixie stuck to Jane like a burr. She stayed on Jane's far side as though I might eat her if she got too close. Maybe I sound like the Buckinghams to her. I have never scared anybody before.

I feel sorry for her but she is a bit babyish.

By the time we got home, she was beginning to skip and giggle though. She and Jane and Sam chattered away about the ocean voyage. It got pretty boring. Sam went over to Robbie's the minute we got home.

Finally I left Jane and Pixie to play with paper dolls

and wrote some in you, Diary. I hate the way paper dolls' clothes keep falling off. There should be a better way to make them stay on than those little fold-over paper tabs on the shoulders.

I wish Barbara was home. I am not jealous! I am lonely. 　　　　　　　　　　　　　　　　·

Bedtime

Pixie looked a lot better when Dad took her home after supper. I think he offered so he could see what he thought of the Buckinghams. He came back shaking his head but he kept mum until Jane and I went up to bed. I sneaked out in the hall then and tried to eavesdrop, but all I heard was, "You were right as usual, Ellen. It's criminal to leave a child with her. She has enough to bear with her own . . . "

He shut the door then, but I think he said the Buckingham twins were "roughnecks." Jane says the boys are mean. She got Pixie to show Sam and me scabbed knees and a lump on the back of her head. She was proud of them, as if they were war wounds. Afterwards Sam told me he thought Pixie was pretty gutsy.

"Well, of course," I said. "It's what your dad told you. The British are the bravest of the brave!"

He stared at me for a moment, as though I were talking Chinese. Then he laughed. "She's a bit small to be all that brave," he said.

Saturday, August 17, 1940

Mother has offered to keep Pixie here half days until she starts kindergarten in September. So there is another WG in our house.

Neither of them feels like the sister I hoped I would get.

Well, I am growing to like Jane. But she does insist on talking about Pixie. She asks me if I think Pixie is beautiful and then waits for my answer. Finally, Diary, I figured out what she is hoping to hear.

"Your eyes are such a bright blue," I said. "Much nicer than hers. And you have dimples. I wish I had them."

She grinned like the Cheshire Cat and said, "Dimples are nothing special, Charlotte. Mummy has dimples."

But afterwards, she kept poking her fingertip into her dimples as though she wanted to be sure they were still there.

Sunday, August 18, 1940

George came home and went to church with us. Mother was so proud walking up the aisle with him. She did not say so, of course, but it shone out of her like giant sunbeams.

Pixie says George is a prince. He thinks she is "a little darling." Ugh! He carries her around on his shoulders. I could tell Jane was not too happy about this. I know how she felt.

It is mysterious how mixed-up feelings get. You would think you could say to yourself, "I will be happy today," and then you could be that way. But it doesn't work. Feelings just flip over into their opposite before you can blink. One minute you feel friendly and in charge, the next you want to yell or hit somebody. I hope this gets better as you grow up. It must.

Wednesday, August 21, 1940

I have a cold. Pixie had it first.

We went to the doctor. When he stuck the tongue depressor in, Pixie gagged and then she kicked the doctor. It was embarrassing!

We got to make Jell-O when we got home. It had only half set when Pixie went back to the kitchen, got a spoon and started to eat it. Thank goodness Mother caught her in time to save some. I love Jell-O. The little pig was not the only one with a sore throat.

Friday, August 30, 1940

I have been too sick to write, dear Diary. My sore throat has gone away at last. Not the throat but the soreness. Now I just have the sniffles. Colds in summer should be against the law.

Saturday, August 31, 1940

It is almost time to start back to school. I did not think about it much until Barbara arrived home from camp. She is very brown and changed somehow. She had lipstick on when she came over but she washed it off before Mother could see. She has a great tan and she has had her hair cut. She is trying to act older, I guess. I hope she gets over this.

They called her Barbie at camp. I don't think it suits her. We have a book that tells about names and hers comes from the same root as "barbarian" and means savage. Savage or not, I am glad she is back. I will have someone my own age to talk to.

SEPTEMBER

Monday, September 2, 1940

Today is Labour Day and tomorrow Central School will be waiting to welcome us. Even though I love summer, I always like the first day of school. Everything seems so new and you never know who might be in your class or who your teacher will be. Also you get new clothes. I have a pleated plaid skirt and a green blouse that matches the green stripe in the skirt.

It will be Pixie's first day in kindergarten. Sam should be in Grade Seven, same as me, I guess. He seems ahead of that though. Jane is the right age to be in Grade Three, but she is also very smart. We'll see.

Barbara does not like Pixie. Surprise, surprise! I actually found myself telling her that I thought the child was pretty cute.

Tuesday, September 3, 1940

School began this morning. Sam is in my class. He was in the Grade Six classroom until recess and then he came in with us. I guess they were trying to see where he would fit. You can tell the teacher likes him.

Jane can read anything and do arithmetic that I just learned last year. And she has the neatest handwriting. It looks as good as Mother's. Before the day was done, they moved her up into Grade Four. She and Sam both seem to fit in so far.

My teacher is Miss McColl and she is lovely. She does want us to do decimals and percents though. She gave us memory work to learn. I love learning poems. Jane cannot understand this. I like having them in my head where I can think about them any time. Miss McColl let us choose and I picked "The Daffodils" by William Wordsworth. I wanted it because I like it, but also because Mother learned it for memory work when she was my age. She recites it every spring.

Wednesday, September 4, 1940

They are planning a concert in the park to raise money for The Cause. Miss McColl said they want children to sing. I would like to try although I never did such a thing before. Miss McColl says Jane and I could sing a duet. Maybe "There'll Always Be an England." I told her Jane absolutely hates that song. They were forever having to sing it on the way over and in Toronto too.

Miss McColl said to ask her and, if she wants to do it, let her pick what we should sing. When I told Jane, she said we should do it. Then she looked sort of sheepish and said she would not mind singing "There'll Always Be an England" now that she has had a rest from being made to sing it. I'm glad because I already know all the words.

Thursday, September 5, 1940

Got in trouble today for passing a note from Sam to Keith Maloney. All I did was hand it on. I thought Miss McColl was fair, but she must have been in a bad mood. She said she should keep me in after four.

Then Sam put up his hand and told her he had written the note and passing it on was not my fault. I was amazed. I don't think any of the other boys would have confessed. The teacher we had last year would have given him the strap.

Then Miss McColl laughed and said we could forget it this time. After all, it wasn't a hanging offense.

I wonder why she changed her mind. I'll bet it was the way Sam looked at her. Nobody likes picking on a War Guest kid. Sam says she is a brick.

Friday, September 6, 1940

Sam got a letter from Terry — the tall boy we saw at Hart House. He hates the people he lives with and he wants to go home to England. His brother has joined up and he thinks his parents need him. He hates Canada.

Sam shook his head over the letter and said he would write back and see if he could persuade Terry to keep trying.

I wonder if Sam himself feels that way at times.

Jane and I are going to sing a duet at the bandstand in Exhibition Park a week from Sunday. We're doing "There'll Always Be an England" and, if they want two, "Bless 'Em All." Jane says it is different singing it with just me. On the ship, they all had to sing at once and a lady kept saying to sing out so they bellowed it.

I pretend I am not nervous. Dear Diary, guess what? I am VERY nervous. Shaking like junket. Wish me luck.

Sunday, September 8, 1940

We went to church and the minister prayed for the people in England who are suffering from bombing raids. Jane had gone downstairs with the Junior Congregation before that, but Sam was sitting with us and I could see him clenching his fists until his knuckles were white. Ministers should think about who is listening before they pray that way. Dad put his hand on the back of Sam's neck and sort of shook it and Sam smiled a little. Dad has a comforting hand.

Sam stayed home from Sunday School. I did not tell. Neither did Jane.

Monday, September 9, 1940

The news from England is terrible. The Germans bombed London yesterday for HOURS. Their planes kept coming in droves, Dad said. People have to go underground in air-raid shelters.

Thank goodness Jane and Sam are safe with us. Sam told us that some of the families in their neighbourhood had dug air-raid shelters. They are like little houses, only sunk in the ground with earth on top of the roof. I cannot picture them. The Brownings don't have one but the people next door do, and they can go in with them if there is a raid.

The Brownings' neighbours have only three people in their family. They put food in the shelter and water and flashlights and a battery radio and all sorts of things. I could tell that Sam wished he could be there with them because he stopped talking about it all at once and ran back to the Bennetts' without saying goodbye.

Sam seems to worry about the milk-wagon horses as much as the people. Jane told me he can calm them when they grow nervous. "Our dad says Sam speaks Horse," she said. "They will be so frightened when there are loud noises and fires."

I wish Jane had not said this about the horses, because I started to think about them and all the other animals in England who must be afraid but do not understand what is happening. Lots of pets must be killed or lost or injured. Not just pets either. Cows and sheep. Pigs too. Grandfather Twiss says pigs are highly intelligent creatures, but they won't understand bombs.

What happens to the animals in zoos? They are trapped in cages and can't escape. I had a hard time not talking about this.

George is home and he got so upset over the news that he began shouting about how terrible it all was. Finally Dad took him into his study. My dumb brother was as bad as the minister. Sam was not there to hear him, but Jane started to cry.

Tuesday, September 10, 1940

They are still bombing London. They call it the Blitz. It comes from the German word *blitzkrieg*. I don't know what it means exactly and it is not in my dictionary.

George will soon be finished at the farm. Then he will go to university. I wish he did not have to leave again so soon.

Jane and I are practising our song for the concert. Pixie keeps coming into our room and joining in — always off tune.

I dreamt about the bombing, and animals running through fire. I woke up crying. Thank goodness Jane slept through this. I don't know what I would have told her when she asked what was wrong.

Wednesday, September 11, 1940

I went to my first CGIT meeting tonight. I had to explain to Jane that CGIT means Canadian Girls in Training. They just have Girl Guides in England. I wore Eleanor's old middy and felt proud that I looked right. I already knew the Purpose too. From now on, I promised to "Cherish Health, Seek Truth, Know God and Serve Others." It was lots of fun. We played games and had a singsong, and the leaders, Miss Walton and Mrs. Jones, led us in a worship service. I met a girl there who seems like a friend already although she goes to Victory. Her name is Beth Fielding.

Thursday, September 12, 1940

Aunt Carrie came over with a couple of her friends. When they heard Pixie singing with us one of them declared she was "so cunning" and we must make it a trio instead of a duet. The other woman agreed. Nobody seemed to notice that the cunning child sings off-key. Nobody asked me what I thought.

We have to dress in red, white and blue and they said Pixie could hold up the Union Jack. I offered to hold up the Canadian flag.

"You don't quite understand, Charleen," one of them said.

I told her my name was Charlotte, not Charleen, and almost walked out. Pixie not only sings off-key but she forgets the words.

Then the same woman asked the other one if she didn't think the two smaller girls made an adorable picture by themselves. The other one murmured something but then Aunt Carrie said firmly, "Charlotte and Jane carry the melody. If the two of them were not strong singers, nobody would hear Penelope."

Aunt Carrie called me a strong singer! I almost fainted from the shock. Thank you, Aunt Carrie.

Friday, September 13, 1940

I got interrupted last night so did not finish what I was writing. After Aunt C's friends left, Mother said, "Carrie's right. You are the one who carries the tune. Without you, the other two would be lost. What's more, you sound as though you mean every word. You sing with your whole heart and you make me cry, Charlotte Mary."

Aunt Carrie nodded. "I don't know why, but you make me see that little cottage beside the country lane and . . . well, your mother's right. You sing as though you mean it, as though you've been there."

I didn't tell her but, when I sing that bit, I always picture the cottage where Martha and Dickon and their mother live in *The Secret Garden*. I have been there, in my mind.

Saturday, September 14, 1940

Too nervous to write. I wonder how many people will come. We had to practise "Bless 'Em All" too, in case they want an encore. I asked how we would know, and Mother said if they kept clapping. Sam promised Jane he would clap like crazy even if he was the only one.

Sunday, September 15, 1940

We did it! And they did want an encore. We sang at three o'clock, right after a pipe band played "Scotland the Brave." They clapped so hard Sam did not have to keep them going. There were hordes of people. Well, at least fifty. Pixie waved her flag so wildly she hit poor Jane on the ear. But Mother said she was proud of all three of us.

It was nerve-wracking though. I do not want to be a famous singer or actress. I would soon have no finger-nails left.

Bedtime

After the concert we went for a family walk and collected milkweed pods for The Cause. They are used, they say, to stuff lifejackets. I am not sure this is true. But we came home with five bags full. It is hard to believe a sailor might be in the ocean wearing a lifejacket filled with milkweed silk from here.

I have known people to collect stamps and butterflies and old coins, but only in wartime do you collect milkweed pods, scrap paper and flattened tin cans.

Monday, September 16, 1940

Nothing to report today, dear Diary, except that Miss McColl told me we sang superbly.

I am teaching the WG kids Canadian songs. They know "O Canada," of course. I thought about teaching them "Land of Hope and Glory," but I went over the words and it is not about Canada but about England. Sam already knows it. We know a lot of British songs, when you come to think about it. Last year we learned "Do You Ken John Peel?" and "Flow Gently, Sweet Afton" at school. I taught them "The Maple Leaf Forever" and "Land of the Silver Birch."

Tuesday, September 17, 1940

George has registered at U of T but he came home again to get stuff for his room in residence. He has the blue and white streamers and a big pennant, and you should hear him singing "Toronto is our University!"

Sometimes he is so nice. He sat next to Jane after supper and drew whatever she asked for. A cow, a leaping deer, a flying dragon. He can draw anything! He always puts in funny bits, which she loves. Jane Browning is not the only one with a good brother.

Wednesday, September 18, 1940

Totally boring day. Jane fell off her bike but she did not hurt herself. She had to swerve fast because she did not see a car turning. The man in the car swore at her though, and made her cry. Some people are horrible.

Thursday, September 19, 1940

Dad is teaching me to play cribbage. He will not play it on Sundays. His mother called playing cards "the Devil's notebook." Mother says it is because people use playing cards to gamble.

Had johnnycake for supper. I am glad maple syrup is not scarce.

Friday, September 20, 1940

Jane has been vanishing into the toolshed and today we found out why. She had a cat hidden away out there, a most peculiar stray. Mother noticed food disappearing first. Jane wept buckets until Mother said we could keep the cat if she settles down. Jane wanted her to sleep in our room but Mother said no, so Britty sleeps in the basement.

We thought Jane was calling her "Pretty," but it turns out Britty is short for Britannia. Britty Kitty. When Sam laughed, Jane was outraged. But she forgave him when Britty rubbed against his ankles and purred.

The school nurse tested our eyes last week and sent home a note to say she thinks Jane needs glasses. Mother took her to the eye doctor and the nurse was right. Glasses are on order for Jane Browning. I thought she would be upset, but she is not. Her mother wears glasses and so does her cousin Hilary. Jane can hardly wait until they are ready.

Saturday, September 21, 1940

We went to Monkey Bridge and had a picnic. Yum. We made dampers out of tea biscuit which you cook over the fire. Then, when they get brown and puffy, you pull them off the stick and fill the hole with butter and jam. They are not easy to get right but they are delicious. Sam and Robbie came. It was a bit strange but fun. Usually George is the one who builds the fire, but we managed.

Sunday, September 22, 1940

I am too tired to write. Besides, I want to read instead. Sorry, Diary.

Monday, September 23, 1940

Another totally boring day. I messed up my Math test and got 13 out of 100. They are going to get me a tutor, they say. I DO NOT WANT A TUTOR. I guess I will have to study and not just copy Barbara's homework.

Barbara is so pleased with herself when she gets every answer right. She has never failed or even done poorly on any test. I think this is bad for her character. It makes her smug.

I must remember to get a Current Event out of the paper tomorrow. I keep forgetting. I would ask Dad to help but he'd make me take a dozen.

Wednesday, September 25, 1940

I can hardly bear to write this. It is by far the worst thing yet. Today we heard that a ship called the *City of Benares*, which was bringing more British children to Canada, was sunk and a lot of the people were drowned. It happened a week ago, but was only in the news today. More than eighty children died! It sounded like Jane's nightmare about being lost on the ship, only it was not a dream. It was real. Every time I remember, I feel sick. I wish I could not see it in my mind.

George came in looking white and furious and so sad. He started in on the ship sinking. When Jane burst into tears, he went out the door with a bang and he has not come home. Where is he? Mother and Dad look sick with worry.

After midnight, September 26, I guess

He came in at last. I heard the front door shut. George never can shut a door quietly. And then I heard voices so I crept halfway down to listen. I think George has enlisted. I am not positive. I didn't dare stay on the stairs once I heard Mother start to cry. But now I definitely cannot sleep, so I thought I would prop up the flashlight and tell you, dear Diary.

This is history happening. George does not seem grown-up enough though to go off to war and help make history.

Jane will wake up if I don't turn off the flashlight. I feel as though I won't sleep but I probably will.

Still Thursday, September 26, 1940

George enlisted in the Navy. He said he was not the only man there who had not intended to enlist until he was through school, but had to go after reading about the children who died when the *City of Benares* sank. He said he also could not stop thinking about the Blitz.

Mother keeps crying. It is strange. She will cry reading a sad book, but she hardly ever cries about real things that are happening. She just gets busy trying to help. But George signing up to go into danger is different. He's still barely eighteen.

When Mother was in tears at breakfast, Jane went over and hugged her. It gave me a queer feeling. She is my mother, not Jane's. I almost went and shoved her away, but then Mother looked over at me. I could tell she knew how I was feeling. She wiped her eyes, hugged Jane back and then blew me a kiss. How can she always know?

George will be in uniform soon and marching in parades maybe and training and then going to sea. That sounds totally unreal. I feel proud of him and afraid for him. I can't believe though that anything really bad could happen to Georgie-porgie. Mother calls him the Artful Dodger because he can always duck out of trouble. But the sea is filled with German warships and sub-marines.

I wish he had flat feet.

Friday, September 27, 1940

Mother has given up knitting for soldiers overseas and is busy preparing things for George. He will have the best socks of any sailor.

Barbara's cousin Daniel, the one in the Air Force, has written to her. He sounds more like a tourist than a bomber pilot. He tells about going to see Buckingham Palace and Kew Gardens. He has been to see Charles Dickens' house. I can't imagine George doing that. But George will be at sea. Barbara says Dan is like a big brother to her. He is nice, but a real big brother matters more.

Saturday, September 28, 1940

They found some survivors in a lifeboat from the *City of Benares*. BUT SO MANY DIED.

The strange thing is that, after a few minutes I forget, and there I am laughing at Dagwood or at something Jane says. I feel so guilty I can't keep laughing. But if I start thinking about how it must have been for those children when they were plunged into the sea, I can't sleep. Even at school, it haunts me.

Yet it also seems unreal an hour later. Mother says

we could not bear living if we had to realize all people's suffering all the time. We would crumble under the weight of it and be no use to anyone. I know she is right, but I also know she has trouble sleeping herself sometimes. She goes downstairs and makes herself a cup of tea. In the morning, I see the cup upside down on the drainboard and know.

Monday, September 30, 1940

George has his Navy uniform. He looks too splendid to be George, except for the ears. He has gone to the base now for his training. I would have joined the Air Force, but George says he has always wanted to see the world and you wouldn't see much from the sky. I remembered then that bombers kill people and innocent animals. I think George couldn't do that. There won't be dogs or babies at sea, just submarines.

Jane and I go around singing "All the Nice Girls Love a Sailor." Mother taught it to us.

When George left, he refused to allow us all to come to the station to see him off. We had to say goodbye at home. He was sure we would embarrass him by making a scene. He lined us up to be kissed and told us we could cry when he actually went to sea. We were laughing by the time he and Dad left.

Sometimes laughing feels like crying.

OCTOBER

Tuesday, October 1, 1940

Every night, after I turn out the light, I sing Jane a lullaby. Then I start the music box. She gets upset if I try to escape without singing. She's a good little kid. I am sure glad she was sent to us and not Pixie. P is not so bad but Jane feels like my sister now.

Wednesday, October 2, 1940

A letter came today from Mrs. Browning to Mother and Mrs. Bennett. She said she had felt badly about sending the children away but now she knows she did the right thing. There was an air raid and a bomb fell on their house. It went right through Sam's bedroom ceiling. The rest of the house is okay but his room was in a built-on bit at the back. Nobody was hurt but the bomb destroyed everything of Sam's. She said that Sam would have been killed for sure if he had been in his bed. *I thank God and you that my children are safe even though I do miss them so,* she wrote.

I felt really queer when Mother stopped reading. She passed the letter to Sam and he read it over and over. He looked pale. I have never noticed anyone actually going white like that, but Sam did.

Then Jane said, "Your planes . . . ! Oh, Sam, your planes!"

And Sam ran out of the house and did not come back for ages. Jane explained that, in his bedroom, Sam had a whole fleet of model planes he had made. They hung from the ceiling on threads. Each one was different. He was extremely proud of them. I suppose he must have thought of them right away. Poor Sam. Now I know why he is always checking the paper for news of the RAF pilots.

But what a lucky escape too. That is what Dad said. And Sam can make new models.

Later

I told Jane we should get Sam a model to start on a new collection. She stared at me as though I had said we ought to adopt a giraffe.

"They weren't just any models," she said. Then she explained that he made his first one when he was just seven. Their grandfather helped but Sam actually did it. He spent ages on each one. No two are the same. "You don't understand, Charlotte," she finished up. "They don't do things like that here in Canada."

Some do. But nobody in our family ever did. Those planes must have taken hours and hours of Sam's life. Days. New ones will be nice, but never the same.

There is nothing that I have done that couldn't be

easily replaced. I don't think I could ever stick at something that way. I am terrible at sewing. I can draw trees but not people or animals. And I've told you about my knitting.

Sam and I are planning to go out collecting old newspapers soon. Robbie might come too. That way we could fill two wagons. I am not sure what good they will be, but the authorities want them. Old metal too. All sorts of junk.

They even want bones! Those can be made into glue for airplanes. Aunt Carrie is actually collecting bones. Trust her.

Friday, October 4, 1940

The fall leaves are beautiful and Jane loves crunching through them. We raked up huge piles and jumped into them last night. Then I taught Jane how to make them into a leaf house. She liked it a lot but had to get Pixie into the game as though it was her idea, not mine.

Do you know about leaf houses, Diary? You rake out square green rooms and hallways and you make piles of leaves for beds and things. Sometimes I get a real blanket and pillow because they make better beds than just leaves. Mother showed me how to make leaf houses when I was about Pixie's age. She said her mother had shown her.

We're going to see *Snow White and the Seven Dwarfs*

tomorrow. I hope Jane likes it and is not too scared by the witch.

Barbara's family is all upset about the French passing laws against Jews. I don't understand why they would do this. People like the Steiners are perfectly fine people. I'll have to ask Dad.

Saturday, October 5, 1940

We went to *Snow White*. Both Brownings and Robbie and Pixie and me without any adult! It made Sam and me seem like parents. That is what I felt anyway. I did not mention this to Sam.

I was glad when Mother said we could go, because the mail from England had made the kids homesick. When she said we could all go to the movie show, everyone cheered up. It was wonderful except that Jane was scared to death by the witch. I don't blame her. She was terrifying. Lots of children cried when Snow White bit the apple. One little girl screamed at her, "Don't eat it!" But Snow White went right ahead and bit into it. Jane put her head face down on my lap and I had to keep patting her back and saying "It's only a story." I sounded like my mother!

The other cartoons were good, especially *Ferdinand the Bull*.

Jane keeps humming "Someday My Prince Will Come" but Sam sings "Whistle While You Work." The Seven Dwarfs were so funny. They all just fitted their names.

Sunday, October 6, 1940

Sam showed me another letter from Terry. It explains why he was so moody lately. Terry does not write much but he sounds absolutely miserable. It is hard on Sam. Terry is in a house on the far side of Toronto. The family make fun of his accent and tell him he must learn to fit in. The advice sounds okay but the people sound mean. Sam will write again but we cannot go to see Terry. He begs Sam to invite him for a visit. Sam says he can't ask the Bennetts. He didn't say why but I think he's afraid Mr. Bennett would be mad at Terry for not being grateful to the people who took him in. I know what he means. Robbie's father is tougher than mine. I think Sam hopes Mother and Dad will help and he wants me to ask. I guess I will, but I did not much like the look of Terry that time we met. I remember being glad he was not our War Guest.

A boy named Lorne something is in the hospital because he climbed away up a pole and touched his head to a live wire and burned his scalp and fell and broke bones. Dad made us all come and listen to the story from the paper. As if we would ever be so dumb! Well, I certainly would not. Sam and Robbie had funny looks on their faces. Boys are weird.

Monday, October 7, 1940

I made Sam show Mother and Dad Terry's letter. They said they would see what they could do. They both feel sorry for Terry. I can't see how they can fix things, but it is nice that they will try. I have great parents, dear Diary, and I know it.

Jane says Terry is grouchy and an awful tease. He did not want to come to Canada. He told them his mother insisted, but his father said going to Canada is running away just when your country needs you. Jane thinks he made poor Terry feel ashamed.

The *Mercury* said that last week the Germans dropped bombs on England from above the clouds. The British soldiers could not see the planes and so could not shoot at them properly. It sounds too terrifying to think about so I won't.

Barbara's parents are worried about relatives they have in France. Maybe it is because of those laws I wrote about before. I asked Dad and I still don't really understand it but Dad says our government should take in more refugees. I am putting this in partly because of Barbara and partly because Dad feels I ought to include historic events in my journal. It should have a sense of this particular time, he says. Almost all of them are sad though. Isn't history ever happy?

Tuesday, October 8, 1940

Terry is coming next week for Thanksgiving. Mother telephoned. She said Terry's people said yes before she had finished telling them why she was calling. They told her he was proving to be quite a problem and they could all do with a break. Sam and Jane are pleased he is coming, but not ecstatic. Jane says he is "not an easy boy" — whatever that means. I guess I'll soon find out for myself.

He is coming on the train and Sam is coming over to stay at our house while he is here. Robbie will miss Sam, I bet, but our families are having Thanksgiving dinner together.

We might have trouble being thankful for three whole days with this problem boy. I will do my best, Diary, but I keep remembering how he scowled at us in Toronto.

Friday, October 11, 1940

George wrote to say he is training hard and will soon be off on his travels. He could not say more because the letters are censored. He makes it sound like a spree. I think he must be scared but not letting it show because of Mother. I'm scared for him.

Terry arrives tonight. This week has been busy, but nothing has happened that asked to be written down. Dad is taking Sam to the train station to meet Terry.

Bedtime

He came. He only had a duffel bag. His face is covered with pimples and the people have cut his hair in a crewcut, like a soldier. It looks ugly. He and Sam are across the hall but I do not think he is asleep. If he weren't fourteen, I would think he was crying. Sam is sound asleep. How do I know which one is Sam? I know because I can hear Terry saying, "Sam, are you asleep?" Sam just goes on breathing and does not answer.

Before we went to bed, Terry hardly spoke. He just grunts! I know I should like him but I can't. I do feel sorry for him. As Mother says, imagine having to BE him. But I hope he cheers up tomorrow.

"I think he is missing home, Charlotte," Jane told me just before she fell asleep.

Her voice was small and lonely, as though she felt that way herself lots of times. And now I am feeling lonely too.

Saturday, October 12, 1940

We went on another family picnic to Monkey Bridge tonight. It is so nice there. It was a bit chilly but we built a big campfire and toasted marshmallows. Terry was not quite so grouchy, although he still had hardly a word to say for himself. He burned his marshmallows on purpose. He said he liked them that way.

They don't have Thanksgiving in England. They have Harvest Festival instead, which sounds like the same thing but not on the same day. They don't have a turkey dinner or pumpkin pie. We are having Thanksgiving Dinner tomorrow and the Bennetts are coming. Terry has never tasted pumpkin pie. Neither have the Brownings.

It was dark by the time we got home from Monkey Bridge and we wished on the first star. We are so lucky to be able to enjoy the beauty of the night without having to be afraid an air raid is coming.

Sam slept over again because of Terry.

Sunday, October 13, 1940

Jane loves pumpkin pie but both the boys thought it tasted terrible. Sam tried hard to eat his but Terry almost spat out the one little bite he took. Then he swallowed it down with a big gulp of water. He actually said, "Ugh!"

Robbie's mother said she thinks they eat pumpkin pie in Heaven. Then Terry amazed us by saying no. In Heaven, they eat bread. He quoted that hymn that says, "Bread of Heaven, bread of Heaven, feed me till I want no more." Everyone stared at him and he went red and shut up like a clam for the rest of the meal.

Jane told me later that his family are Plymouth Brothers or something. He goes to "chapel" and he knows lots of hymns and Bible verses. On the ship coming over, when they sang hymns or spirituals, Terry always knew the words without looking at the song sheet. Sam and Jane are Church of England, which is like our Anglicans. They don't have The United Church of Canada there, of course. That is our church and it is three churches that came together, the Presbyterian, the Methodist and the Congregational. Some Presbyterians stayed out. Hey, Diary, I bet you didn't know that. I learned it at Sunday School.

The boys went off on bikes after dinner. Terry borrowed Mr. Bennett's bicycle. I wanted to go too but I was not invited. Pixie came over to play with Jane. Barbara and her family went to Toronto to be with their family. I admit it, dear Diary. I felt left out and sorry for myself. But when they came back, Sam looked as though it had not been fun, and Terry was growling and scowling.

One moment showed me a different Terry, though. We were listening to the radio and watching the fire in the fireplace. Britty had wandered in and, without anyone noticing, she jumped onto Terry's lap. She usually only goes to Jane. Next thing I saw him stroking her and actually smiling. His lips moved and I could see he was saying, "Puss-puss, pretty Britty puss." And she purred like a locomotive. It didn't last long but he certainly seemed like a much nicer boy for those minutes. Then he saw me watching him and gave me a dirty look.

Britty jumped down as though she could tell she was about to get shoved off his knee.

His train goes tomorrow after lunch and I am counting the hours.

Monday, October 14, 1940

Today was nice because there was no school. But everyone missed George. And somehow we couldn't talk about him in front of Terry. I don't know why. I think we were afraid of what he might say or maybe of showing our own feelings. He came down for breakfast carrying his duffle bag all packed and he hardly spoke a word all morning. It was not a thankful day until Dad took him to the station. We didn't do anything all that special, just played crokinole and Parcheesi. But everyone felt happy.

Tuesday, October 15, 1940

I felt guilty when we came home from school and I was glad Terry wasn't here. When his name came up, Mother looked worried and said, "I hope the visit helped the poor lad, but I think he is truly unhappy here."

"We can't fix things," Dad said. "He'll have to work it out for himself."

Sam thinks Terry is worried about his brother, who is in the Army now. I am worried about my brother, so I ought to be more sympathetic.

Wednesday, October 16, 1940

We had a great time at CGIT. I picked up Beth
Fielding on the way and we walked there together.
Beth loaned me a book called *Sue Barton, Student
Nurse*. I like it too much. I just read another two chap-
ters even though am supposed to be studying for a
Math test.

Thursday, October 17, 1940

Today, right after school, Sam and I got ready to go
on our paper drive. Just as we were setting out, Barbara
arrived with her wagon and asked to come too. She did
not tell us her wagon was a disaster.

Anyway, we were given huge piles of newspapers. We
tied them up in bundles and tied them onto the wagons. We brought the first load home and stacked it in
the garage and set out in the opposite direction. We
were blocks from home on our second run when it
began to get dark and we tried to hurry but we couldn't
go too fast with our heaped-up wagons.

We filled Barbara's last and this was the moment
when one of its front wheels started going sideways and
sticking. Sam got down and straightened it again and
again while Barbara just stood there, looking helpless.

Since it was dark, we walked her home first. Sam was
dragging her dumb wagon for her. Her mother heard us
and came out mad as a hornet. Then Barbara cried and

actually told her mother that she had not wanted to go, but Sam had made her. Her mother glared at poor Sam and yanked Barbara into the house and slammed the door. When I think how much easier it would have been without her, it makes my blood boil. I began to tell Sam I was sorry but he just started pulling that wagon around to their garage.

The schools are holding a contest to see which one collects most. With Sam driving us on, Central will win for sure. We won't take Barbara again.

We were in trouble coming home so late but Mother and Dad calmed down when they heard where we'd been. We are to get home before dark next time.

Friday, October 18, 1940

Barbara came up to me this morning and pretended nothing was wrong. I just stood and stared at her and did not speak until she went red and muttered that she was sorry. I was going to ask her why she lied, but I didn't because I know why. She is afraid of her mother. How horrible that must be! I cannot imagine feeling that way about mine. I told her to forget it, but I don't think either of us will. Sam won't, that is for sure.

The Steiners are really worried about what is happening to the Jews in Europe and Barbara is terrified that her cousin's plane will be shot down. But I can't see that this is any reason to be mean to us. I'm worried about George, but it doesn't change how I act toward Barbara.

Saturday, October 19, 1940

I'm supposed to be cleaning up my room but I need to write in you, I really do. Besides, our room looks fine to me.

I'm finished the first Sue Barton. Beth has more books about her. I can hardly wait.

Now that Barbara is home and school is taking up my time too, I have to force myself to write in you, dear Diary. But I must not stop. I know starting up again is much harder if you stop.

Barbara came over after lunch and wanted to talk about movie stars. Jane followed us and sat down on the bed and Barbara told her this was a discussion for older kids and she should go and find someone her own age to play with. Jane left without a word.

I told Barbara that this is Jane's room as much as mine and she should not speak to her like that.

Then Barbara said she felt sorry for me, being stuck with Jane. She went on to say she thought Jane was babyish and she didn't like her prissy way of talking.

I wanted to hit her. I feel as though Jane is my true little sister and Barbara is someone I used to like long, long ago.

What is more, Jane is not babyish. She's just young.

She looks good in her glasses. She loves them so much she hates taking them off to sleep.

Barbara left in a huff. I am sorry, but she is rubbing me the wrong way these days. Yet she is still my best friend.

Sunday, October 20, 1940

Still mad at Barbara. Tried to get over it. Didn't. Church did not help.

Monday, October 21, 1940

Nothing to write unless you want to hear about how I almost got 100 on my English Composition. I lost two marks for saying "Everyone got their lunches." I still think "THEIR lunches" sounds right. Miss McColl said the story itself was EXCELLENT.

Mother told me, in secret, that she is afraid Britty is pregnant. I was thrilled until I thought about what would happen to the kittens. Maybe we can find them homes. Jane will break her heart over giving them up. I hope Mother is wrong this once.

Wednesday, October 23, 1940

We are going to have a CGIT Hallowe'en party the night after Hallowe'en and invite our younger sisters. I will bring Jane. After we came home, I told her and she is all excited about the party.

I am glad I am not as old as Eleanor. She only dresses up if she goes to a masquerade party. It sounds exciting, but to me Hallowe'en still means going out into the dark in a costume and going from house to house saying "Trick or treat."

I have thought of a couple of different costumes, but I must match up with Jane somehow. She wants to take Pixie! I think Pixie is a bit young but Mother says she has the clown costume I wore when I was five. So that stopped my objecting. She WILL make a cute clown. And she likes doing what we do.

Thursday, October 24, 1940

Sam got another letter from Terry. Terry keeps saying he will run away. He heard that his brother is missing in action. I hated reading that letter, but I really cannot see how we can help. Sam knew we couldn't, but he still feels terrible.

I read Jane "Little Orphan Annie" from our poem book last night. She loved it until I turned out the light. Then she shivered and shrieked and pretended goblins were all over our house.

Saturday, October 26, 1940

We are gathering stuff for our costumes. Pixie is a clown, of course, so we decided we would all be from the circus. Jane is going as a trapeze artist and I am going as the ringmaster, in Dad's top hat and carrying Eleanor's whip from when she had riding lessons. Jane says I should take a chair and be a lion tamer but then the boys heard what we were planning and now Sam is being a lion tamer, with Robbie being a tiger in their tiger-skin rug. The head is really ferocious, with long yellow teeth and glass eyes that look menacing.

I wish it was ours. I like lying on it and stroking its head despite its fierce expression.

Sunday, October 27, 1940

We went to church and Sunday School, of course. They asked me to help out with Jane's class because the teacher had a headache. Jane positively beamed. Except for that grin, it was a dull day.

Monday, October 28, 1940

I wish Hallowe'en would hurry up and come! Lizby made lemon snow pudding tonight. We have not had it for ages. Yummy! It is the custard sauce that makes it so good. We got some extra eggs given to us by the people George worked for in the summer.

Tuesday, October 29, 1940

Tonight we carved wonderful jack-o'-lanterns to put in front of our houses. Robbie and Sam did theirs at the same time. Sam made a scowling one. Mine is grinning and has a tooth missing. Mr. Bennett brought home a skeleton he borrowed from his nephew. It is not a real one, but it looks great. They have it hanging in the hall with candles lighting it up. It is enough to make a little kid faint dead away on the doorstep.

Dad helped Pixie do one of the pumpkins. She was so pleased. She kept beaming up at him as though he was her fairy godfather.

Wednesday, October 30, 1940

Barbara came over to see my costume. We are friends again although we are still a bit stiff.

Mother has made homemade fudge to pass out and taffy apples and balls of caramel corn. There are lots of candy kisses too in their orange and black paper. I like them especially. Maybe I like them so much because you can't get them any other time of year. They are like hot cross buns or Christmas cookies.

Hallowe'en, Thursday, October 31, 1940

After school

We can't go out until we have had supper, but I am too excited to read or even listen to the radio. Our costumes are magnificent. Mother found a ballerina dress for Jane and sewed spangles all over it. She made her a headdress too, with ribbons that will float when she swings through the air. I am wearing George's church suit and Father's tall hat and Eleanor's riding boots, which I said fit me although they are really a bit too big. Mother found me a fake moustache to stick on.

Barbara would not come with us when she found out I would be going out early with Jane and Pixie. She thinks you should only go when it is pitch dark. The little girls are so excited that I catch it from them.

Much later

Jane is asleep with her hair still spangled and with candy apple around her mouth. Dad carried her up and put her into bed without waking her.

We had lots of fun and got heaps of candy. Mother lets us eat all we want, which is wonderful. Barbara's mother takes hers away and hands them out two a day for ages. You would think it was her candy, not Barbara's. She went out with Janny and Marlene. I think it is the only night all year she can go out at night without a grown-up.

NOVEMBER

Friday, November 1, 1940

We went to the CGIT Hallowe'en party with our little sisters along. It was fun but I am too tired to write about it. We wore our same costumes. Beth went as Santa Claus! Jane was much better behaved than some of the other girls' little sisters. Goodnight.

Saturday, November 2, 1940

I am in a writing mood!

Winter is almost here. I wonder what Jane will think of our snow. They do have some snow in England, but not like ours. We do not live in an igloo, but Canada is "the true North strong and free." Jane probably does not know about snow angels and building forts and things like that.

Jane's birthday is on Tuesday. A parcel arrived for her from England today. I am so glad. It would be terrible if there had been no present from home for her. I am giving her BALLET SHOES and a baby doll with a nightgown and a blanket. I wish it could be a rubber doll she could bathe, but there will not be any of those until the War is over. Mother says she misses elastic most. Doing up your underpants with a button feels risky.

George asked Mother to get some sparklers for Jane so it will be like Guy Fawkes' Night in England. Sam has not told me what he is giving her. He laughs and says it will be a big surprise.

Some more British expressions

lorry: truck
pudding: dessert (We have pudding for dessert lots of times, but Sam and Jane call cake and pie *pudding* too.)
Harvest festival: Thanksgiving
jersey: pullover sweater
joint: roast
paddle: wade

Bedtime

Lizby made a cake today and forgot to turn the oven from pre-heat to bake. The cake came out about an inch high. Lizby cried. But it was for the church, not Jane's birthday. Jane and I ate it before Lizby could throw it out. It was kind of crunchy but we liked it.

Aunt Carrie is knitting Jane a sort of dress. It has a pullover top in stripes and under it a top like an undershirt sewn onto a skirt which is all blue and sort of rippled up and down.

I would hate it but Mother told Aunt Carrie that Jane would love it. I gave her a look that said she was crazy if she really believed that, and she shook her head at me ever so slightly and tightened her lips against a smile. Maybe Jane will surprise us.

Mother got her *The Five Little Peppers and How They Grew*. It is long but Jane likes reading. Mother also got her a new book of paper dolls with fancy old-fashioned dresses. There are even bonnets and a muff. Jane will love them. So will her pal Pixie.

Monday, November 4, 1940

We are in bed already, Diary, because Jane told me we had to go to bed early so her birthday will come faster. She said she would not be able to sleep if I didn't come too. She fell asleep in eleven minutes, but now I am up here I might as well stay. She has been torn all day between missing her mother and bubbling over with excitement because her birthday is tomorrow. Being a WG is complicated.

Tuesday, November 5, 1940

Jane's birthday and Guy Fawkes' Day

What a splendid day! Jane loves her doll. She named her Mary Charlotte after me, but she just calls her Mary. Jane and Mary are both in the bed and Jane is sound asleep. Mary is gazing at me. Her eyes don't shut. I have a doll whose eyes do, but they click every time and it spoils the effect.

George sent her one of his funny cards. He drew a picture of her in enormous glasses. Over her head was a label saying SPECTACULAR JANE. It took me a minute to get it. George is so smart.

Sam's surprise was a Guy made out of old stockings

and pillows. It has yarn hair and a painted-on face which is lumpy because of the stuffing. He and Robbie had made a big bonfire behind the Bennetts' and we went over and danced around it waving sparklers.

Pixie was invited for the whole party, but that aunt came and took her home before the fire was even going. Never mind. Pixie got the dime in the cake and she was pleased as punch.

Barbara came over for the bonfire and she gave Jane a package of gum. Jane loves gum. Mrs. Steiner thinks it is "vulgar" for a girl to chew gum, so Barbara only chews it at our house.

Jane actually did like her knitted suit! She gave Aunt Carrie a kiss! Aunt C positively beamed at her. I guess making that suit was a lot of work. That's what Mother said. I'm glad Aunt C made it for Jane and not for me.

Grandpa gave her a brand new dollar bill. That is a lot of money when your allowance is 10¢.

Wednesday, November 6, 1940

Now Jane's birthday is over and we can start looking forward to Christmas. I wonder where George will be then. It will be so strange not having him with us. He has always been the life of the party, hanging up mistletoe in the kitchen doorway and kissing Mother every time he caught her coming in or out. He gave joke presents too, fake teeth and rubber spiders and a paste-on moustache. That was for Eleanor. It was in her stocking, but we all knew George was the Santa who put it there. I can't bear to think of Christmas without him.

Thursday, November 7, 1940

We got a letter from George. He seems to be drilling night and day. They found out he can play the trumpet, so now he is in the marching band. He says we should hear him play "Rule, Britannia." I did not know sailors marched. He complained about it, but I bet he was really pleased.

We are starting to gather things to go in Christmas boxes for the Brownings and our sailor boy. I am going to buy him a harmonica so he will have something to play when he is not marching. Mother is making peanut brittle for him.

Friday, November 8, 1940

Barbara was saying nasty things about Jane again today and I told her that I didn't want her coming over if she was going to be mean. Jane never comes near us now and I know her feelings are hurt. Barbara does get jealous but somehow, right now, there seems to be more to it. She got up to go without a word and then sat down and hid her face in her hands. I waited for her to explain. She didn't. So I said, "Forget it." I showed her a new sweater that Mother got me and then she left.

I wish I understood what is making her so touchy.

Saturday, November 9, 1940

Mother made me clean our room today. Jane was supposed to help but Pixie came and the help vanished. When I complained, Mother looked at me as though I were being horrible. She said I should stop grousing and try doing my share. It is Jane's mess as much as mine, Diary. And I don't think I was grousing! Grrrr!

Sunday, November 10, 1940

Britty was missing this morning. We had to leave for church without knowing where she was. Jane was frantic. She actually cried because she was sure Britty had been stolen. Nobody would steal Britty! She is nice once you know her, but she is the homeliest cat in the world.

When we got home, Jane finally spotted her on the roof of a house two doors down from ours. She was crouched down by the chimney, calling pitifully for rescue. It took ages and many people to get her down but, in the end, Sam went up the ladder after her. Was she grateful? She scratched him right across the chin. But Jane thought her brother, the cat rescuer, was braver than Superman.

Jane and Sam's grandfather writes reports about her

Scottie dog in England. So far Skippy is fine but Jane still worries about him. Her grandfather numbers the letters and a couple had never arrived. They might come later, of course. Sometimes that happens.

It is hard for Sam and Jane writing letters home, not knowing if they will make it there. The Brownings love getting news though, so the kids keep at it.

Monday, November 11, 1940

This is Remembrance Day. We had a special assembly at school and I recited "In Flanders Fields." Dr. John McCrae, the author, was from Guelph. My grandpa knew him. Jane and Sam were amazed by this because they studied the poem in their school in England. Then Dad told us it was published first in England in *Punch* magazine. Sam liked that.

I like the larks in the poem. They fly "still bravely singing." I can hardly believe this bit, but I hope it is true.

One of the teachers played "The Last Post" on his bugle. It is so sad. They talked about the grave of the Unknown Soldier. I did not let myself think of George.

Tuesday, November 12, 1940

Dear Diary, are you feeling neglected? There is a lot of work for school these days. It is as though the teachers think we have to learn everything before Christmas.

They are also starting to plan Christmas concerts and decorations.

We all have to write a composition called "Why I Love Canada." Miss McColl suggested some of us might like to write a poem about this. Everyone groaned but I wonder if I could do it. I had a small idea about how it would end, but a small idea is not a poem.

I did ask Dad about why the Nazis hate the Jews. He was quiet for ages, thinking, and then he said he could not explain it to me. I would have to wait until I was older. I told him that I hated it when adults say that. He smiled at me and said he knew how I felt, but he was unable to give me a quick answer that would help.

"It isn't that I am hiding some truth from you, Charlotte," he said. "It is that I myself cannot fathom such inhumanity."

Then he gave a big sigh and said he had to go. I think this is the only time I can remember his not being able to explain something to me. I wonder if Barbara understands. I wish I could ask but I can't. All I know for sure is that it is crazy.

Wednesday, November 13, 1940

I am reading Jane *Rebecca of Sunnybrook Farm*. She is sad for Rebecca, who is sent away from home just like her. But then Rebecca makes us laugh with her chatter.

Thursday, November 14, 1940

We are getting new dresses for Christmas. Mother saw some she liked in Budds. Jane is hoping for red velvet. Red velvet would be nice.

Friday night, November 15, 1940

Coventry was bombed last night. It was a terrible raid, the paper said. We have no word about Jane and Sam's grandparents or Jane's dog. Jane was right to be worried. They bombed Coventry Cathedral, which was old and beautiful. Dad said it was an outrage.

Sam came over before school to be with us and wait for news. Dad thinks the Brownings will send word tomorrow. People talked about the bombing on the radio. It sounded awful. Not just awful. Wicked!

You would think, if the Germans had to bomb a place, they would try not to hit a church. I was thinking that they would not have cathedrals in Germany, but Dad says they have lots of them. The Church of Our Lady, right here in Guelph, is a copy of a European cathedral.

Mother sent us to school because it would help to pass the time until we got word from England. At recess I found out that Jane was crying her heart out. I asked if I could take her home. She was better as soon as she reached Mother. I wanted to stay but I went back.

Saturday, November 16, 1940

We got a telegram. Sam and Jane's grandparents were in London and so were not home during the raid, but their cottage had a direct hit. They cannot find Jane's dog but they are still looking. It is lucky that it is Saturday, because Jane has done nothing but cry or curl up in a ball of misery since we heard. The cable said LETTER FOLLOWING.

God should stop things like this from happening. I told Mother and she said, "How?" I don't know the answer but I still think He should.

Jane is heartsick about her missing dog. I keep saying I am sure he is fine, but my being sure is no help.

I will read to her. She can read herself, but she likes sharing a book, laughing at the funny bits and talking it over. I like it too even though I am twelve.

Sunday, November 17, 1940

There were some survivors in Coventry. It was on the news on the radio. It does not mention dogs, of course. Dad and Eleanor went to church but Mother and Jane and I stayed home. It is so hard, dear Diary, waiting. We spent most of the afternoon finishing *Rebecca*. It is nice because there is no war in it.

Just before supper, Jane suddenly started crying again. It was not about her dog but about all the special things in her grandparents' cottage that must have been lost. Here are some of them: Grandpa's rocking chair, a big teapot with flowers on it, her grandmother's embroidery frame.

Jane has a petit-point picture her grandmother did for her of a tree with a pony under it. The stitches are so small Jane calls them "mouse stitches."

Her grandpa made a bookcase that has books in both sides and turns around on something like a Lazy Susan. I told her I had never seen one like that and she said of course not. He invented it! He also has a bunch of walking sticks that stand by the door in a thing like an elephant's foot. He has collected them from around the world.

What was worst of all was when she told about their hundreds of books. Some were so special. When she started to name some, like all the Andrew Lang fairy books and *The Lost Prince* and a big stack of Christmas Annuals, we cried. It was like learning of the death of friends.

Monday, November 18, 1940

When I told Barbara about Jane's crying and worrying about Skippy, she was truly sorry and that made me feel better about her. She is not as heartless as I was starting to believe. Also, I think now some of her dislike of the WGs is connected to those Jewish children her family could not get out of Europe. Maybe she is angry that Jane and Sam are safe with us while those Jewish children are still in danger. I do not understand what could be happening to children, except getting bombed. I can't ask Barbara. She would have told me already if she wanted to talk about it.

Tuesday, November 19, 1940

We still have no good news about Skippy.

I am trying to write about loving Canada but it is not easy. It keeps sounding dumb. I was telling Sam and he offered to help. It turns out he really likes writing poetry. He felt he couldn't say he loved Canada yet, but he might help me. I jumped at it. We asked Miss McColl if the two of us could do it. She said that would be great.

Wednesday, November 20, 1940

Sam and I are hard at work. I think it might be good. I hope so anyway. Sam is a good writer.

No word about Jane's dog, but it is too early for a letter about him to reach us anyway.

Thursday, November 21, 1940

Our poem is done, dear Diary, and I'll write a copy on one of your pages. I hope I can make it look beautiful. I can't use carbon paper. It looks so smudgy.

Here it is. I admit that the best lines are Sam's, but the idea is mine and I wrote most of the first and last verses.

Why We Love Canada

We love this land, our Canada,
Her people clean and strong.
With steadfast hearts and smiling eyes,
Through life we march along.

We children here in Canada
Are taught to think ahead,
And build a land of peace wherein
To earn our daily bread.

Her mountains rise magnificent,
Their snowy peaks aloof.
Great ocean breakers wash her shores.
The far blue sky's her roof.

Her summer is a golden song,
Her autumn crisp and bright,
Her spring all green awakening,
Her winter cold and white.

We stand on guard for Canada.
Our young men go to war
To keep the country that we love
Safe from shore to shore.

Her streets are filled with noisy life.
How still the prairie's space.
Sometimes it seems that Canada's
A mirror for God's face.

He's surely proud of Canada,
Though many things we lack.
When He looks down on us, God smiles
And Canada smiles back.

It still sounds rough in spots, but Sam and I are proud of it. We will show it to Miss McColl tomorrow. I can hardly wait.

Friday, November 22, 1940

Miss McColl was away today so she won't see our poem until next week.

There was no news from England. I keep picturing Jane's dog coming safely home. I pray I am right. If Skip turns up, I think they'll send a telegram because they will know how Jane is worrying.

Mother let Sam help her fill the bird feeder today.

He is fascinated by the birds. They are different from British birds. He says our robin is not a robin at all, not like the robin in *The Secret Garden*. I would like to argue with him but I know he is right. At the feeder now are mostly chickadees and sparrows.

Pixie loves the chickadees and Jane says that Pixie would be one if she were a bird. I asked her what the rest of us would be. Then she said I would be a nuthatch because I do things upside down. Sam would be a woodpecker. George would be a bluejay. And Eleanor would be an owl, a small one. Jane would not explain. But I loved watching her seriously deciding.

Saturday, November 23, 1940

It is hard longing for news from England and yet knowing it is too early for a letter to come.

Jane droops and you can see her sort of shrinking. Even having Pixie over does not help. I can't bear it. But I have no way to stop.

Sunday, November 24, 1940

Waiting, waiting. It was a terribly long day.

Monday, November 25, 1940

We got scrappy letters from George. We don't know where he is, though we assume he is on his ship by now. Sometimes bits are blacked out by the censor.

He's not supposed to leak information. It seems sense-less. We do not know any spies! All he has told us is that he is always cold.

Bombing is still going on. I cannot bear to write about it. I found out what *blitzkrieg* means. Lightning and thunder.

Tuesday, November 26, 1940

Skippy is alive! Jane got a telegram from her grandpa. LETTER ALREADY ON ITS WAY, it said. But he is alive!

Miss McColl loved our poem! She wants us to make a scroll with our poem written out in fancy lettering. She will hang it on the wall. Sam says he can do the lettering.

He and Jane got more mail from England. It is queer when you really think about it. They feel happy because their family is safe. But they might NOT be safe by the time the letters reach us. I wish I had not thought this. I'll bet Sam has figured it out, but not Jane. Skippy is her one worry.

Wednesday, November 27, 1940

Jane is sick. She woke me up wheezing and she stayed home from school. She looks miserable. Her cheeks are flushed and she has a high fever. When Dad came home, he called Dr. Steiner, who said to keep her drinking and he'd be right over. She is in her bed and I am staying with her even though she seems asleep most of the time.

Thursday, November 28, 1940

I can't write with Jane so sick. Oh, Dear diary, what if she does not get better? Every so often, she cries a little and says, "Mummy. I want Mummy." It is awful. She seems so sick.

Even reminding her that Skippy is alive only brings a flicker of a smile.

Friday, November 29, 1940

It is not full morning yet. Jane has pneumonia!! Dr. Steiner put her in the hospital last night. Everyone is worried. Sam looks almost as sick as she does. Her breathing sounded as though every breath hurt. She just lay there, no word or smile.

Saturday, November 30, 1940

I got thinking about pneumonia in the night. I have read books where children died of pneumonia. Jane's mother is so far off. Mother has decided to wait a day and see if Jane is any better before she writes Mrs. B.

Dr. Steiner told Dad there is a new drug, a "wonder drug" they call it. It has not been used much yet, but he thinks it may make a great difference. It has a long name but it is called Sulfa for short.

When he talks about this, he looks even more excited than Robbie with Mackintosh's Toffee. His eyes positively shine and he can't stand still. I wanted to go to the hospital to visit Jane but they would not let me. They said she is too sick for visitors.

DECEMBER

Sunday, December 1, 1940

Jane's grandpa's letter telling about Skippy finally arrived today. He sent it airmail. I thought it might be one of the letters that gets lost on the way because of the War, but I was wrong. He wrote it a couple of days before he sent the telegram and then he realized Jane should not have to wait for such good news.

The dog came to the bombed cottage and a friend saw him and called them to come and pick him up. He was missing for two days but then he came limping home. He had a cut paw and he is a bit bruised but he'll recover, her grandfather says. Mother took the letter to the hospital. Jane is terribly anxious about the limp and those bruises but the rest of us heaved sighs of thankfulness.

There is lovely deep snow. It looks Christmassy. But, in spite of the news about Skippy, our house feels empty without Jane. You would think I would enjoy having my room to myself again, but it feels too quiet and lonely without Janie. I'll be so glad when she comes home.

Her grandparents have moved in with Jane's parents. I hope it is safer there. I don't see how they can sleep at night, imagining bombs raining down. But you have to sleep!

Monday, December 2, 1940

The Sulfa drug is making Janie better. Mother says it is a miracle. Dr. Steiner says it is called a miracle drug, that it will save thousands of lives. They have written the Brownings about her being sick, now that they can say she is getting better.

Even Barbara is pleased. I think she has come around to really liking Jane. This is a great relief to me. I hated being pulled apart by them. She is also proud that her father was able to get the miracle drug for Jane. It is still very new.

The school concert is coming. Sam has printed our poem out and I am to read it aloud. Jane's class is to sing "The Campbells Are Coming." She was excited about it and now she might even be well enough to go. It is still more than a week away.

Sam told me that what he really wants for Christmas is a typewriter. I don't know anyone our age with one and he said he knew he would not get it. But I told Dad in secret and Dad thinks he might get him a second-hand one. I must not tell in case it doesn't come true. I hope it does. Sam deserves it.

He asked me what I wanted myself. I told him as long as I got a new book, I did not care. Grandpa will give me theatre tickets as usual. You can go to six movies with them, whichever ones you choose.

Mother found a perfect book for Jane. It is meant for grown-ups, I think, but it is about a dog. *Jock the Scot.* It is a British story, which is another reason Mother got it. It is by Alice Grant Rosman. It is a love story and a dog story both. I love it.

Tuesday, December 3, 1940

Jane is coming home tomorrow. I can hardly wait.

Eleanor is actually knitting her a pair of bedroom slippers. They are red and white with tassles. All those socks she knitted have made her an expert.

Britty keeps searching for Jane, mewing and mewing. I thought cats did not care about people much, but Britty proved me wrong.

Wednesday, December 11, 1940

Dear Diary, I am too busy to write. I promise I will be back. Jane is still not healthy and there is so much to do for Christmas.

Friday, December 20, 1940

We are out of school and the Christmas holidays have begun! I know, Diary. I skipped days and days. But I have been so busy reading to Jane when she came home from the hospital, and then getting ready for Christmas. Once you stop writing, I find, it is easy to stay stopped. But I am starting again. Eleanor asked me how I was getting along with keeping my record of my thirteenth year and I said it was going fine. But I went red, Diary. Telling Eleanor a fib is not easy because she is such a good person.

Just four more days until Christmas!

Monday, December 23, 1940

Just two more days now!

We are joining together with the Bennetts and having dinner at both our houses. We are doing the first part and they are providing the dessert. Aunt Carrie and Grandpa will be coming over, of course.

I think Christmas is making the WGs excited and terribly homesick both, although neither of them is saying much. At home they put real candles on their tree, and the parents send the kids out and decorate it without their help. When Sam and Jane first see it, it looks glorious, they say. Also, they hang their stockings up at the foot of the beds, while we hang ours at the fireplace all in a row. We will have to decide what to do.

They also call Santa Claus Father Christmas. He has a lot of names. Kris Kringle and St. Nicholas, for two. They are different and yet they are the same. I think every one of them has a beard though.

Tuesday morning, December 24, 1940

It is Christmas Eve Day. I always think I will not live through the hours and hours until Christmas actually comes and then, suddenly, it is here and it flashes past much too fast. One thing that helps to stretch it out is reading Christmas stories like *The Other Wise Man* and *The Birds' Christmas Carol*.

We've decided to hang our stockings on the beds but bring them down to the fireplace when we wake up. Jane says it isn't right, but that is what we have planned. Sam says he is too old to have a Christmas stocking, but nobody gets that old at our house, not even Grandpa. When he and Aunt Carrie come over for dinner, we'll have his stocking ready and waiting. Aunt Carrie's too, even though she says it is foolishness. And Sam's.

Sam told me that he has not had a letter from Terry for more than two weeks and he is a bit worried. I hope Terry is just too busy and happy to write, but that sounds unlikely.

Christmas Morning

Wednesday, December 25, 1940

Merry Christmas, dear Diary. Everyone is still asleep. It is not light yet. Dad said no getting up until six, and so I am waiting for Jane to wake up on her own. After all, she still seems too thin and pale. Oh good. Here comes Britty, meowing. Well done, Brit.

Bedtime

Christmas is over and we are in bed. We all missed George terribly. At least we know he got his parcel.

I did get a good book. It is a beautiful copy of *A Little Princess*. I have read it, of course, but Mother knew I would love to have it for my very own. I have it here and I am going to read it by the light coming in from the hall until I fall asleep. Downstairs, on the radio, an English boys' choir is singing Christmas carols. It sounds like angel voices.

Did I say how thrilled Sam was when he saw the typewriter? He was thunderstruck.

Boxing Day

Thursday, December 26, 1940

The phone rang before sunrise this morning. It was the police. Terry is missing. The people who got him think he might have been going to find Sam. But nobody knows where he is. Sam does not know either, of course, but he was right to be worried. I wish we could search for Terry, but the police are doing that. We are supposed to call them if he shows up.

What if he has frozen to death somewhere? What if we never find him?

Friday, December 27, 1940

No news of Terry. I don't like him, but I keep remembering him petting Britty. By the way, she is definitely pregnant. Jane is thrilled! Mother is not.

Please, Terry, be all right.

Saturday, December 28, 1940

The doorbell rang this morning and a policeman was there with Terry! He looked terrible. He was dirty and half frozen. His nose was running and he glared at us as though he hated us. Then Mother stepped forward and wrapped her arms around him and he burst out crying in big gulps.

"I'll see to him," she said. Then she looked at Dad and he nodded and went to fetch Sam. They can talk without saying a word.

She took Terry away and ran him a hot bath and told him to wash his hair. When he was finished, she handed him in some clothes of George's and then fed him breakfast. He wolfed down the food using both hands to shovel it in. I guess he had had hardly anything since he ran away.

We were sitting at the kitchen table with him when he burst out, "If you send me back, I'll run away again the first chance I get."

He wants to go home, bombs or no bombs. Sam asked what Terry thought his parents would say. Terry showed us a crumpled letter from his dad saying he wished he had kept him home. Dad read it but he did not say anything.

Then Terry told us that his older brother Alan is still missing. He heard just before he ran away. He did not tell the family he was sent to live with. He said they would not care and I thought he might be going to cry.

Nobody knows what to do, but Mother said Terry can stay with us for now.

"Until we get it sorted out," Dad said.

We are all glad T is safe but he is still not easy to have around. It is like having a little, sharp pebble in your shoe which keeps poking into you. You could stop to get the pebble out but Terry just goes on making you limp.

Sunday, December 29, 1940

I can't write anything. Everything is so muddled. Jane keeps crying, and Terry looks like a thundercloud most of the time. Even Mother can't smooth down his prickles. She keeps trying but it isn't easy. It is like trying to pet a growling dog who sounds ready to bite.

Monday, December 30, 1940

Britty has had two kittens! One was dead but the other is healthy as can be. Jane said Terry could name him and he said he would call the kitten Sabretooth. Jane did not like that at all, so Terry changed to calling him Pouncer. Jane did not like that much better, but we are trying to live with it. The kitten being born helped cheer everyone up. You do understand, Diary, that this kitten is too small to pounce or do much but drink and squeak.

New Year's Eve
December 31, 1940

One wonderful thing has happened during the last few weeks. Pixie's "auntie" has started to grow fond of her. They actually took her to the Santa Claus parade in Toronto and then to Eaton's Toyland. She sat on Santa's lap! They got her a doll buggy for a present. Pixie will positively love pushing it up and down the sidewalk when the snow is gone. Dad found a cradle for her and Mother has made a mattress and pillow and quilt for it.

Aunt Carrie had made her a Raggedy Ann doll. You can never tell with Aunt Carrie.

If only Terry would try to fit in and be content. But he must be frantic with worry about Alan. I wonder if "missing" really means Alan must have died. I pray not. Sam says he might have been taken prisoner by the Germans. He thinks that might be worse than dying. Sam is wrong about this. Terry's family must want him alive whatever happens.

This is the last day of 1940, dear Diary. What a surprising year it has been! It is hard to believe that a year ago I did not know Sam or Jane or Pixie or Terry or Miss McColl or Beth. It makes you wonder what is coming next.

1941

JANUARY

New Year's Day

Wednesday, January 1, 1941

Did I tell you I got a new dress for Christmas, Diary? I guess not. Terry's being lost put it out of my mind.

It is lovely. It is deep blue velveteen. Jane got one too. Hers is red velvet with a Peter Pan collar. We feel splendid when we put them on. We have all been invited to a Twelfth Night Party at the Bennetts', and we will wear our new dresses. I've never been to a Twelfth Night Party before. Mrs. Bennett said she refused to let Hitler rob us of celebration and festivity. The boys make rude faces when anyone speaks of it, but I know they are pleased underneath.

Twelfth Night is next Sunday, really, but the party will be on Saturday night.

Thursday, January 2, 1941

Mother told us at breakfast that she has been asked to go back to teaching AND they have given her a class in our school so she will be close to home, which is nice. What's more, it is Jane's class. Her teacher enlisted during the holidays, leaving them short. I wish I had had Mother for a teacher.

It will feel weird to meet her in the hall as we come and go.

Jane is pleased as punch about this. She burst out with, "You won't put all the names on the board for the money, will you? It makes Natalie cry."

It took quite a while to get that mystery cleared up. It seems that Jane's teacher puts every child's name on the board on Monday mornings. When you bring in your 25¢ for a War Savings Stamp, your name will be erased. Natalie's father died a year ago so her mother is raising the five kids on her own. She never has a quarter to spare for a War Savings Stamp. When the names are mostly rubbed out, the teacher makes the ones who have not brought money come up in front of the class and lectures them about the War Effort.

"I gave her my birthday money from Grandpa," Jane said. "And Redge gave Monty some he had. She makes them feel awful."

Mother and Dad thought this was terrible, but at least that teacher has gone now. Lizby was furious. She knows how it feels to be looked down on because you are poor.

"You can bet your life I will do no such thing," Mother told Jane. "You should have told me about this before, honey. I could have spoken to the principal."

Diary, why are some people so unfeeling and others kind right through? I could feel how ashamed Natalie must have felt every Monday. Jane's eyes went round at the idea of Mother talking to the principal. She and Sam call him the headmaster.

I have books filled with the stamps. When the War is over, we will get our money back and more besides. I will be rich. But only after we win the War.

Bedtime

Terry got another letter. It was sent on from the place where he lived. His brother IS a prisoner of war! Sam was here and the three of us were talking about the War. Sam said something about "when we win the War" and Terry said, "What if we lose, Sam? Did you ever think of that? We could, you know."

I could not believe my ears. I am sure he does not mean it. How could we lose?

His sister is working as a Land Girl. Men who used to work for farmers have joined up and girls are taking their place. Terry says it is back-breaking work. His sister's name is Betty and she sounds nice. When Terry talks about her, his eyes sort of light up.

The grown-ups are still discussing what to do about him. Terry's father said he wishes Terry could be sent home. *I could do with his help here,* he said.

And he'll want him more now they know about his brother.

Friday, January 3, 1941

Every time I write 1941, it surprises me.

We were tobogganing all afternoon. Terry forgot to be a grouch and had loads of fun. He ran over me with the toboggan once, but the snow was so deep I sank into it and was not hurt a bit. I think he was terrified he had killed me. When I stood up, covered with snow, he whooped with relief.

Tomorrow is the party. I hope it is really fun.

I especially hope it will make Terry feel better.

Lately, he stays off by himself and hardly speaks to anyone. Sam gets him to come over to the Bennetts' and they stay in his room with the door shut. Robbie listens but he says they don't talk much. Sam lets Terry work with him on his model planes.

What will happen to him? Will he have a little fun at the party? I hope he doesn't ruin it somehow.

Saturday, January 4, 1941

The Twelfth Night Party is right after supper. It is hard to think of going to a party when you are also thinking of Terry's brother being a prisoner.

It feels like a tug-of-war. On one end of the rope is the Brownings being in danger, not knowing where George is, thinking of those Jewish children Barbara worries about, remembering the *City of Benares* sinking and Coventry Cathedral being bombed. The thought of so much danger and hurt pulls at me, dragging me over into sadness and worry. But on the other end of the rope are Britty and her kitten, good books to read, the poem Sam and I wrote, pulling Christmas crackers, and writing in you, dear Diary. These happy things drag me back to safety. Sometimes it feels as though I just catch my breath and then I am being hauled away again.

But tonight is the party! I'll concentrate on that.

Bedtime

What a wonderful time we had! There was a big cake filled with good things we have not tasted in ages. Mrs. Bennett saved up and got people to donate dates and nuts and lots of butter and sugar. There was somebody dressed up as The Fool who went around playing little teasing tricks on people. He put an ice cube down my neck! We were told when we got there that nobody was to mention the War. It was a relief to hear no bad news all evening. We sang every verse of "Green Grow the Rushes-O" and I remembered all the words and never forgot where we were. I saw Terry sitting in the corner by the door, where he could get away if it got too bad, I guess, and he was singing! It was glorious sung by so many voices.

We all got small special presents. Jane's was a tiny glass tea set almost too small for a doll to use. There are two cups, two saucers, a sugar bowl and a cream pitcher. They fit into a little cardboard box. Mine is a tiny deck of cards with pictures of birds on the backs. Mother says they are for playing Patience. Her mother had those tiny cards and she called the game Patience too, although nowadays we say Solitaire.

Jane says in England they still say "Patience." Maybe I will add it to my word list.

The boys got whistles and little spinning tops that really spin.

Sunday, January 5, 1941

Somebody threw a rock through the Muellers' store windows. It has happened before, but this time they have closed the shop, boarded up the windows and moved to Toronto, where they have relatives, I think. Mother went over the moment she heard, but they had already gone. She came back in tears and Eleanor had to get supper.

Terry hates the Germans enough to do something like that, but he is too happy to have done it this time. He is going home next week. His father and mine arranged it somehow. Even Terry's pimples look happier. Sam is happier too. Terry was a big worry to him.

I asked Sam if he wished he was going home too and he said of course he did. Then he looked straight at me and said, "But only partly. I'm used to being here now. I'm learning to play hockey. Sometimes here feels more like home than there does."

Then he turned and ran off as though he felt guilty for what he had said. He is caught in the tug-of-war even more than I am. Much more, I guess.

Jane told me that she is afraid she is forgetting her parents' faces. I found the pictures her mother sent, but she says they do not look like themselves in black and white.

Later

I wonder if Robbie will be happy that Terry is going home. Sam will spend more time with him now. Terry treated Robbie the same way Barbara treated Jane and Pixie at first. Never mind. That's all over.

Monday, January 6, 1941

School started today. It felt so strange with Mother setting out ahead of us. Oh well. It was fun to see everybody and we will begin going to CGIT again.

I hardly see Barbara over Christmas because her family does other things. I miss her. Sort of. More than sort of. But she was kept home today with a cold. Her mother fusses over her one and only child, just like Britty does with the kitten.

Tuesday, January 7, 1941

Nothing worth writing about. Terry is getting packed to go. School is full of homework. Barbara talks of nothing but her cousin Daniel who is in the Air Force. He could fly before the War started so now he is training pilots. They mostly come to Canada to be trained, she says. I like him but I get tired of her bragging about him as though winning the War is a sure thing with Daniel in charge.

We have heard not a word from George for ages.

Now that he is probably at sea, it makes not hearing from him harder. But he did say he was cold so he must be in our hemisphere. Please, God, keep him safe.

I don't talk to Barbara about him. I am afraid it might bring him bad luck. I know, Diary. That is dumb. But I am a bit dumb now and then.

Wednesday, January 8, 1941

Dad is always watching out for naval reports in the paper or on radio broadcasts but they don't say much. We know there are German U-boats sliding along, searching for ships to sink. They could even come into the harbour at Halifax without being spotted. Our ships often sail in convoys around the big troop ships, trying to sink the German boats before they can break through.

A man Dad talked to sailed on one of the troop ships though. He told Dad it is fearsomely cold and the men suffer terribly from the frigid weather and the rough seas. They all have frostbite, he said. And some of our ships have been sunk! One German ship, the *Bismarck*, has sunk several already.

It is not good news, Diary. Why did he tell us? Mother looked sick.

I do not think Dad should repeat such things. She will picture George freezing to death on some icy deck.

I know she will. Or even worse, of course, in the ocean.

If I remember this at bedtime, I will cry myself to sleep.

Why doesn't George write? I'll bet Mother starts knitting him thicker mittens and heavier socks.

Jane is besotted by Britty's kitten. If she had had more, Mother would have taken them to the Humane Society. But one is possible — especially when we consider how Jane would cry her heart out if she had to say goodbye. She keeps changing his name. At the moment he is Butterball.

Friday, January 10, 1941

Terry has gone. He looked strange when he left. He was happy to be going but I think he had become fond of us, to his own surprise. And, dear Diary, I actually miss him! I would not have believed this was possible. But he got a lot nicer once he knew he was going home.

I hope no submarines are waiting out there while his ship sails across the sea. After all we read and heard about the *City of Benares*, I would be afraid to go.

Sam has not come over since Terry went. I bet he has that tug-of-war feeling. Jane is sucking her thumb again.

Saturday, January 11, 1941

I love Saturdays. It is so nice to be home all day and have Mother home too, even if she does have to plan lessons now. Jane snuggles up beside her on the chesterfield (Jane calls it a sofa) and Mother keeps one arm around her while she writes with the other.

Am I jealous, dear Diary?

Yes!

But Pixie is coming over this afternoon, which will remove Jane to their pretend games. I appreciate Pixie more than I used to. She is growing, for one thing. She is not so skinny and waifish. And she sounds much more Canadian.

Some more of my second language

jolly: very
Father Christmas: Santa Claus
headmaster: principal
Patience: Solitaire
wellies: rubber boots
mackintosh or mack: raincoat
row: argument or quarrel
jersey or jumper: both mean a pullover sweater

Sunday, January 12, 1941

We've been invited to go on a sleigh ride this afternoon. All the WGs and their Canadian families. Even Pixie's auntie has agreed to come. I hope it will be lots of fun. Sam and Jane have never been on a sleigh ride, although they know "Jingle Bells." I can hear Jane singing it downstairs.

"Bells on cocktails ring," she sings. I will have to straighten her out before the boys hear her.

We are all staying home from Sunday School.

Home again, bedtime

I fell off twice but so did Sam. Eleanor slipped once but caught herself. It was really fun. The sleigh bells had belonged to Mr. Wigmore's grandfather and had a wonderfully joyful sound ringing out over the snowy fields. He told us they had rung that way for nearly one hundred years.

Monday, January 13, 1941

We got a letter from George today. The censor let it go without much inking out, which is nice.

He is at sea. He doesn't say where, of course, or tell us the name of his ship. The sea is so big. I bet it isn't a sea but an ocean. He misses us. He has Eleanor's and my pictures up in his locker and he said his friends say we look "smashing." That does not sound like George. Will he come home changed? His best friend's name is Bertie and he's British.

I have made a vow to write more often. George seemed so lonely. He sounded like a man one minute and a boy the next. Mother has the letter in her apron pocket and, whenever she sits down, she reads it again.

Tuesday, January 14, 1941

Sam will be thirteen tomorrow. I got him two Hardy Boys books.

I have started writing more to George, Diary. I think I will skip writing to you sometimes when I write to him. Mother says she will keep me supplied with stamps.

We give half our allowance for War Savings Stamps. We had a big family meeting about this long ago and we all decided it was right. Sometimes I wish we had not made this decision, but back then it seemed great to be noble and give our own money to help.

Wednesday, January 15, 1941

Happy Birthday, Sam Browning. May your 14th year be great!

He liked the books and the cake Mrs. B made. We all went over there for the birthday supper. Great food! Quite a heap of presents! It helps to have two families when your birthday comes. He got a couple of complicated model kits from his grandpa. Jane said she had told him what Sam wanted. I'll bet he knew without telling.

Thursday, January 16, 1941

I wrote to George last night. You have to use flimsy airmail paper that is strange. Your paper is much nicer, Diary. But I have nothing to say today except that the kitten who used to be Butterball is afraid of mice! Britty watched him see one and then back up. Then he rushed forward and made a giant pounce to show her that he knew what he was supposed to do. He totally missed the mouse, which ran off snickering. He is called Only now, short for The One and Only. Only seems to fit him.

Saturday, January 18, 1941

I wonder how long it will be before George realizes what a fabulous sister I am. It is not easy to write when I don't know what he is doing. I just chatter away about the kitten and Pixie's funny ways and what books I am reading.

Here's a good example. Pixie's front tooth came out and you will never guess what she did, Diary. She put it under Jane's pillow instead of her own because she was sure her auntie did not know about the Tooth Fairy.

It was a good thing that Jane told us, or the Tooth Fairy might not have come to our house either. I did not tell one time, and the Tooth Fairy never arrived. Mother blushed and said she could not imagine what that fairy had been up to. The next night, the money arrived with a small note in fairy-size writing. It said, *So Sorry, T.F.*

I think George will like hearing about this.

Wednesday, January 29, 1941

Lizby caught what Aunt Carrie calls The Grippe and Mother calls a Bad Cold. It was not pneumonia, but we were afraid it might turn into something really serious. So I was busy helping much more than usual. I didn't have one minute to write in this diary until today. I actually think I have dishpan hands!

Eleanor might have helped more but she has a lot of homework since she is in Fifth Form.

FEBRUARY

Sunday, February 2, 1941
Groundhog Day

I hope that groundhog does what he is supposed to and makes spring come quicker. I am already fed up with winter. I hate wearing so many more clothes and clumping along in galoshes.

Monday, February 3, 1941

Letter to George Day.

Tuesday, February 4, 1941

George got two of the letters I wrote before New Year's and he sounded so pleased that I was glad I had written them. He likes all the stuff about the cat and Pixie and what we had for dinner and what book I am reading. He says it makes him feel as though he is here with us. He also said he has a friend who thinks Eleanor is beautiful. Eleanor was flattered, I suppose, but not really interested. Yesterday I saw a lipstick in her top drawer. I was not snooping. I was putting her handkerchiefs away. I can't imagine Eleanor in lipstick.

Thank goodness Lizby is better. I actually did learn to iron without scorching things, but it makes me extremely nervous.

Mother is making fudge to send to George and his friends. I wonder if she will have any to spare for the hungry mouths at home. I will at least get to lick the spoon and scrape the last out of the pan.

Friday, February 7, 1941

Marnie Severn was away from school today because her brother was lost at sea. Somebody said that the telegram only said MISSING, but nobody at school knows for sure. I feel terrible, but I keep thinking not of Marnie but of George.

We mailed off another parcel to him yesterday with the candy, more socks and mittens, some film for his camera and some new snapshots of us. There was also some old Cheddar cheese, which he especially likes. It seems a strange thing to send to somebody at sea, but Mother says that she knows George better than I do and he has never not been hungry, especially for cheese.

Saturday, February 8, 1941

Dull, dull, dull.

Sunday, February 9, 1941

Wrote to George. I do not like February. It still seems years until spring dances in.

Monday, February 10, 1941

Maybe I should give up keeping a diary. I seem to have nothing to say. I do have a cold, which might explain it.

Wednesday, February 12, 1941

Wrote to George yesterday. Used up all my writing energy.

Today Jane is all excited. She has made Valentines

for everyone she knows. They are really well done. I think Sam helped a bit. Weeks ago she made one for George and gave it to me to send so he would get it on time. It says, *You are my hero!* He should be thrilled.

Valentine's Day
Friday, February 14, 1941

I watched Jane go off carrying a box filled with Valentines. She walked with me at first, but now she meets her new friend Melissa on the way. I know Ralph Jenson picked on her when school started and made fun of her accent, but she made him a card because nobody likes him. She is a very nice person. Right at this moment, she seems more like my sister than Eleanor does. I hope she gets as many cards as the rest out of the Valentine Box.

Later

I am waiting for Jane to come home. What if nobody gave her a Valentine? Of course they will, but I will be glad when the suspense is over. Oh, here she comes!

Later again

I need not have worried. She came home loaded with Valentines. Ralph gave her one. You are supposed to sign them with a question mark but he wrote his name. She showed me and said he was much nicer than she had thought.

Saturday, February 15, 1941

Jane and I spent all morning pasting all her Valentines into a scrapbook so she "will have them forever." I never had so many. Never mind. I had my share, Diary.

Sunday, February 16, 1941

It was a usual Sunday. We went to church. We went to Sunday School. We wrote to George. We read. It was nice. Peaceful. The way Sunday is supposed to be.

Monday, February 17, 1941

Written at noon

I got a letter from George this morning before I left for school. I brought you with me with the letter tucked into your pages. When I read it at recess, it unsettled me. I don't know how else to put it. His friend Bertie got a letter from some old lady in his home town, telling him that his girl was going out with other men while he was away. The woman said she thought it was her duty to tell him. How can people be so cruel? Mother would call that woman a meddlesome busybody but I think she must be a wicked old witch.

It will be hard to concentrate on schoolwork this afternoon, Diary.

After supper

Another letter from George was waiting for me when I came home. I think he wrote it right after the last one. He says Bertie is heartbroken about his girl being so fickle. He asked if I could talk Eleanor into writing to him. Bertie thinks she is so beautiful and George thinks a letter from her might help him to put his old girl out of his mind.

I am pretty sure Eleanor won't do it. She is too shy and too proper. But I guess I'll try.

Bedtime

I tried talking to Eleanor about Bertie as soon as she came in. I gave her both of George's letters to read. But she said she could not do it. She did not know him. What would she say? Just thinking about it made her panic.

What should I do about Bertie, dear Diary? George enclosed a picture of him. He is not very tall. He has a really nice smile. The picture is black and white, of course, but George says he has brown eyes.

What if he should be killed believing nobody cares about him? What if he gets so depressed he jumps overboard?

Midnight

Jane is sound asleep but I can't stop worrying about Bertie. Is there something I could do? He would not want a letter from me. He would think I am too young to understand.

But I have sat here in bed making up letter after letter in my mind.

Tuesday, February 18, 1941

I spent almost the whole day writing a letter to Bertie in my mind. Then, as soon as I got home, I went upstairs and wrote it down. I can't believe I did it. I kept a copy. I think I might need to keep track of what I said. Here is the letter.

Dear Bertie,

My brother George told me about you and sent me your picture. I maybe should not say this to someone I have never actually met, but I know, from looking at your picture, that you and I could be friends. I wonder if you would enjoy getting letters from a stranger in Canada. If you don't want to hear from me, tell George and he will let me know.

Your would-be friend,
Eleanor Amy Twiss

P.S. This is a picture of me as I look now. The one George has was taken at least a year ago.

Then, dear Diary, I put in a picture of Eleanor with her new haircut and party dress. I knew I would get cold feet if I waited to think about it so I went right out and shoved it in the mailbox before I lost my nerve. Have I done a terrible thing?

Even though you can't talk, Diary, I know you said "Yes."

Wednesday, February 19, 1941

I cannot believe I did what I did. Should I write and try to explain? I can't. Oh, Diary, how could I have been so crazy? This is going to get me into terrible trouble before it is all over.

Thursday, February 20, 1941

I almost told Barbara what I had done, but at the last minute I got cold feet and buttoned my lip, as Grandpa would say. I could not face hearing her telling me what she thought. I am sure she would be horrified.

And she just might spread the word around. I don't think she would, but I did not tell, just in case.

Thursday, February 27, 1941

I could not write anything all week because every time I opened your pages, I saw the letter. Soon Bertie should have it. And life keeps moving along and I can't desert you, not after nearly nine months.

Every so often I remember what Eleanor said when she gave you to me, and I wonder if I have changed at all. I think I would not have written to Bertie on my last birthday. I don't know what that says about me though. Maybe then I was sensible but timid and now I am senseless but brave. That sounds dumb. But maybe a little bit true.

Will Bertie answer my letter? I don't know what to hope. I wait to snatch up the mail before Eleanor comes in. Luckily she has started to stay at school over the noon hour for special help in French. She is not good at languages. But it is still too soon, really.

Both the morning and afternoon deliveries are here by the time I get home. If no letter is there, I just leave the envelopes on the hall table. So far, there is nothing but it is really too soon. Still, the mail is unpredictable nowadays.

I have homework waiting. I'll be back.

Friday, February 28, 1941

No letter! None from George and none from You-know-who.

Well, I only mailed mine eleven days ago. I should not be expecting to hear back yet.

MARCH

Saturday, March 1, 1941

Spring should come soon. Thank goodness there is no mail on weekends so I can relax. We are going to the show tonight. They say I am finally old enough to go at night. About time!

Sunday, March 2, 1941

Sam has joined the Junior Choir! That Miss Little is so sweet that he could not say no to her any longer. She had already caught me. The Junior Choir doesn't sing all the time but there is special Easter music. We have to sing one anthem in which the chorus starts, "Up from the grave He arose." Sam sings it at anybody he catches lying down.

The mail deliveries start up again tomorrow. Woe is me!

Monday, March 3, 1941

No mail from Bertie.

Tuesday, March 4, 1941

Ditto about letters. Drat. Spring will come and summer and no mail. I am crazy.

Wednesday, March 5, 1941

Nothing from B.

I have a new piece of memory work. It is by Rupert Brooke and is about his maybe dying in the war. One bit goes "that there's some corner in a foreign field that is forever England." It almost makes me burst out crying because it made me think of Bertie talking. Only he wouldn't die in a field but at sea. How can I even think such a thing?

Thursday, March 6, 1941

Can't write today. Am reading to take my mind off it all.

Friday, March 7, 1941

The newspaper tells about the battle in the North Atlantic. Ships are being sunk every day almost. Some are theirs but some are ours. We do not even know the name of the ship George and Bertie are on. I have bad dreams about huge grey ocean waves with icebergs in them crashing into tiny ships and pounding them down. I also had one where there were people lying face down in the ocean and nobody could turn them over. I tried to scream and move but I could not move or make a sound. When I woke up, I could not stop shaking and I was afraid to go back to sleep.

I don't ask, but I do wonder if the others have nightmares too. I hear Jane whimper sometimes and I call her name until she either wakes up or stops.

But there are lots of happy times. Janie got 100 out of 100 on her Arithmetic test last week. She showed it to us, repeating, "Never before! Never before!" Dad asked her what had made the difference and she said, with a grin, "It was my new teacher."

Usually Dad doesn't reward us for getting good marks, but he gave Janie a whole dollar. One hundred cents for one hundred marks. "Don't let this become a habit, miss, or you'll have me in the poorhouse," he said.

"Charlotte told me you don't have a poorhouse here," she said.

I did tell her that after she read a book that had a little girl dying in a poorhouse. Dad just laughed and went back to reading the paper. Later, in private, he told me about the House of Industry, which is on the way to Fergus and is a Canadian poorhouse. He said it was not like the one in Jane's book and he thought I should not tell her about it, in case it worried her.

Dear Diary, if only you could tell me what to do about Bertie. Why did George ask for a letter? I know, Diary. He never meant me to write the way I did. Eleanor was supposed to do it. Whatever possessed me?

Saturday, March 8, 1941

I have been so busy worrying about Bertie that I never wrote that today is Mother's birthday. I got her some Ivory soap, which is a boring present but what she said she wanted. It floats, dear Diary. Did you know that? It is also 99 and 44/100 percent pure! She says she is forever losing the soap in the bathwater. Really!

Sunday, March 9, 1941

At breakfast Mother said she loved her soap, all four cakes. I love her so much. I hope she is telling the truth. I thought I should write her a poem to go with it, but I just could not come up with anything.

The rest of Sunday was as Sunday always is. We had a "day of rest." But inside, I was not resting. Tomorrow there will be mail again. What do I hope for?

That kitten helps. He chased a roll of toilet paper all over the upstairs and it was such a mess that we had to laugh. Laughing felt nice.

Monday, March 10, 1941

Bertie wrote back! Airmail. I got the letter at lunchtime and nobody saw me snatch it up. There was one from George too. I carried it in to the table and then went into the bathroom to read the one addressed to Miss Eleanor A. Twiss. I have never felt so nervous and guilty as I did opening it. Here is what he said, Diary.

Dear Eleanor,

Thank you so much for writing to me. I would really like to get letters from you. I need a friend right now. You are stunning! As we say in the Navy, hubba-hubba! It isn't just the pretty dress or the hairdo either. You have a wonderful smile. It is even sweeter than the candy your mother sent us. Tell her it lasted about three minutes and we LOVED it.

I just put on some warm socks George loaned me, since I have nobody to knit them for me. It is colder than Santa Claus's cellar ▓▓▓▓▓▓▓▓▓▓▓▓▓▓▓▓▓▓ ▓▓▓▓▓▓▓▓▓▓▓▓▓▓▓▓▓▓ *the wind cuts through you as though you had nothing on. Lots of us have frostbite. Chilblains too. But the warmth in your kind words really helped. Please write back to me. I will be watching for your letter, Miss Eleanor Amy Twiss.*

Sincerely,
Bertie Jenson

One part was blacked out. I wonder what it said.

Now what do I do, dear Diary? He sounds so nice. I will have to write again. But what can I say? He trusts me!

No, he trusts *Eleanor.*

I am going to bed even though it is not yet nine o'clock.

Tuesday, March 11, 1941

Yesterday, after I finished talking to you, Diary, I wrote half a million letters and threw every one of them out. I feel terrible about Bertie but I feel terrible about lying to him. I wonder if I could possibly confess to Eleanor and persuade her to do it after all. But when I imagine doing this, I feel sick at my stomach.

Nearly midnight

I finally wrote it all out in a sort of confession and left it on Eleanor's pillow. She has gone to the movies with Susie and Carol.

Diary, I will tell you what happens tomorrow — if she does not kill me.

Wednesday, March 12, 1941

Eleanor is mad as fire. All morning she would not speak to me. All afternoon she was furious. Then she started to cry and I cried too, which helped, I think.

She made me bring her Bertie's letter. I think she might write to him. She said she had to think it over.

If diaries can pray, pray for me, dear Diary.

Thursday, March 13, 1941

Tonight, at supper, Dad quizzed me a little about what is going on in the world. Then he got out the atlas and he made me find places like Yugoslavia and Singapore and Egypt and he told me some of what is going on. Russia too. This war really is a world war. He said I should know more about it. And that when I had to get a Current Event to take to school, I would choose with intelligence. I did not promise, but I will try.

It was hard to think about Egypt when Bertie is taking up all my mind.

Later

Eleanor told me, after supper, that she had written to Bertie. She did not tell him what I had done. She just picked up where I left off. I asked to see the letter and she would not show it to me.

"If I am going to keep it up," she said, "I can't be thinking about what you would think."

I was slightly mad but mostly enormously relieved. I think she plans to go on writing. I hope so. She could not help liking the things he said about her being stunning.

Friday, March 14, 1941

Busy writing to George. The news is frightening and it feels better when I have written. It is as though I know God will save his ship at least until my letter gets there. My fingers are so tired from being crossed all the time, hoping to bring my brother luck.

Later

Sam got a letter from Terry. He has been in several bombing raids, but their house has not been hit. He is happy to be home. They can write to Alan and send packages, but they don't know if he gets the food. His mother says she is glad to have Terry home and she does not know what she would do without him.

After supper

Barbara's cousin Daniel has not written to them and she is worried. If something terrible had happened, they would tell the family right away, wouldn't they?

I am going to finish writing to George now, Diary.

Nearly midnight

I forgot to write that there has been intense bombing of Glasgow, Scotland. I clipped out a bit about it for Current Events. It felt wicked to turn something so terrible into a clipping for school, but Sam brought the same one.

Saturday, March 15, 1941

Today is the Ides of March. It is the date that Julius Caesar was assassinated. Miss McColl told us yesterday. When I told Dad, he said that was true, but that the calendar they used then is not the same as the one we use now. When I asked for more details so I could tell her on Monday, he said he was late and I should look it up. That is irritating!

Barbara said she would call if they heard anything about Daniel. She has not called. He is her cousin, of course, not her brother. But the family would soon hear if the news was bad. She does love him a lot.

It is so hard being afraid of something but not being able to do anything but wait. I hate waiting for anything.

Monday, March 17, 1941

The top of the morning to you, dear Diary. It is St. Patrick's Day and I am wearing my green pullover. I wanted to wear green kneesocks but Mother said not yet. It is maddening. Other girls are changed out of long lisle stockings by now. Not Barbara though. I can count on her mother being fussier than mine.

I made up my mind when I started this diary that I would not write about the weather, but it is hard not to mention that it is beginning to get warmer and you can smell spring coming.

Mother heard a crow this morning. Sam told her that he had seen two of them.

"One for sorrow, two for joy," Mother said.

Sam got this big grin on his face. "My Grandpa says that," he told her. "Three for a girl, four for a boy."

"Five for silver, six for gold," Mother carried on.

Then they finished together. "Seven for a secret that cannot be told."

I wish I knew that secret.

Still no word about Daniel.

Wednesday, March 19, 1941

The Steiners got a letter. Daniel was in France on some sort of mission. He said he enjoyed the milkweed. I think that means he was in the ocean and needed his lifejacket. But he can't tell us details, of course. The censor would just black them out.

Barbara is so relieved and happy. Daniel is nice. He took us out for hot chocolate before he went overseas.

Did I tell you that Lizby did finally decide to enlist but got turned down because of her health. She is too small or something. Mother hugged her and said she thanked God that the armed forces had no sense and let her keep her treasure. "I could not manage this household without you," she said. It is true!

Lizby looked much happier. She has met somebody at her church. He comes around and has a cup of tea with her after we finish the supper dishes. Then they go for walks. He's very shy.

We are all going to a skating carnival next week. It will be at the arena. Jane has never been to such a thing. I bet she loves it.

Friday, March 21, 1941

This is officially the first day of spring. It does not feel like it, although the buds are coming out on the trees. We all went out to the sugar bush the other day to see how they make maple syrup. They don't have sugar maples in England. Mother is sending the Brownings some syrup.

Their grandparents have moved back to Coventry. They are sharing a house with friends or something. Skip stayed in Wembley. Jane had been worried about him being left alone all day because her mother was out driving army officers around, and then she heard back that her mother had stopped driving for the time being and was working at home. Sam said he wondered what kind of work she could be doing but nobody had an answer.

Jane is always so quiet after they get mail from England. Sam is too. I think it brings their parents close and reminds them of the bombs falling. The news is full of disasters. I can't bear to think about it.

If only George had not joined the Navy! All of the armed service men face dangers, I know, but I can't even write down why the ocean seems the worst place to be.

Monday, March 24, 1941

The skating was wonderful. There was this one girl called Barbara Ann Scott who is almost the same age as I am. She was the best skater on the ice! She won something, but being able to skate like that is better than winning. She looked so lovely. She made it look so easy, as though she flew and floated and spun around and around without even having to try.

Now Jane is determined to learn to figure skate. I wish I could, but just plain ordinary skating is more than I can manage. I always end up falling on my bottom. I'll have to read her *Hans Brinker.*

Thursday, March 27, 1941

I am tired. We had choir practice tonight. Miss Little is so nice but she does make us do the songs over and over. "Shoulders back, Charlotte," she says. "Chest out. Head up. Now sing out! We want everyone to hear you."

I do my best, but I feel foolish with everyone staring at me. I wish she would not mention my chest. I have a verse to sing by myself though. So does Sam. She never has to tell him to "sing out" because he does it naturally. He never worries about the audience.

The bravest of the brave.

Saturday, March 29, 1941

We went to see Gracie Fields in *Queen of Hearts* at the Capitol. Dad really likes Gracie Fields. Sam and Jane's father does too. We have a record of her. I like the one about her taking her harp to a party.

Sam told me proudly that the British sank a whole bunch of Italian cruisers and destroyers yesterday. Dad had already told me, but I did not say so.

Monday, March 31, 1941

Eleanor got a letter from Bertie. She said it was private. But I think she was teasing and she will let me read it after she has digested it.

APRIL

Tuesday, April Fool's Day, 1941

Dad played a mean joke on us this morning. He called up that there was no school and then, just as we were starting to cheer, he said, "April Fool." Jane actually laughed at him, which was bad. You should not encourage an adult to think he is funny — even when he is. It goes to their heads.

We gave in our War Savings Certificates at school and they raised more than five thousand dollars for The Cause! Our school raised the most. They are buying five mobile canteens with the money. It is a great idea because the drivers can take the food and stuff right to where it is most needed. The *Mercury* wrote it up, which is great because Sam and Jane can send the clipping home.

Wednesday, April 2, 1941

In the *Guelph Mercury*, it says we will have floods. I would like to live by the river but not to be flooded out.

George wrote and said he was so frozen his eyelashes stuck straight out in little spiky icicles. I wonder what the censor thought of that. George is overly proud of those eyelashes. Maybe the censor just laughed. Censors are people, after all.

Thursday, April 3, 1941

Choir practice again. Easter is just ten days away. It is late and I am going to bed. Homework plus choir is wearing.

Friday, April 4, 1941

It is getting warmer. I have a skipping rope all ready to hand to Jane the minute the sidewalks dry up enough. She can skip but she does not know how to turn Double Dutch. I will teach her. I can't skate but I am a grand skipper. I also know all the rhymes. My own favourite when I was younger was,

Teddy Bear, Teddy Bear, turn around.
Teddy Bear, Teddy Bear, touch the ground.
Teddy Bear, Teddy Bear, say your prayers.
Teddy Bear, Teddy Bear, climb the stairs.
Teddy Bear, Teddy Bear, point your toe.
Teddy Bear, Teddy Bear, out you go.

I wonder if they skip to the same rhymes in England. Somehow I think not. But they do skip. Eleanor Farjeon wrote a story about it.

I also have marbles but I am not as good at them. I love the look of the marbles though, the ones that let the light through and have swirls inside. I like the way they clink together too. And I like having a full-to-bulging bag of them. They are as much a sign of spring as robins or tulips.

The world seems lovely here but Dad and Sam were talking tonight about the British having to retreat from Libya because of General Rommel's troops. Dad said it was too bad Rommel wasn't on our side. I guess he must be a good general.

Do they have tulips and skipping ropes in Libya?

Sunday, April 6, 1941

Today is Palm Sunday. I like the hymns, but it is sad to think of children waving palm branches and cheering when Jesus rode into Jerusalem. They didn't know He would be killed. I wonder if He knew. I hope not.

Dad says He must have had strong hands to be able to control that unbroken donkey.

There are services all week in the evening. Eleanor goes but Mother doesn't expect me to. I like singing in church but my feet get twitchy if the sermon is too long. I like the ministers who tell stories best. You forget the sermon before you get outside, but you remember the stories.

Wednesday, April 9, 1941

We made Easter cards at CGIT for old people who can't come to church any more. We cut out flower shapes and pasted them on. I still have paste under my fingernails but my card looked lovely. Beth made one for her grandmother, who is one of the Shut-Ins. Imagine being known as a Shut-In.

They have started a group of Sea Cadets down in the boathouse at the bottom of the college hill. They will wear sailor suits and drill and learn to tie knots. I was starting to make fun of them until Mother looked at me and I remembered that George is a sailor. I even go around singing "All the nice girls love a sailor."

I don't think Sam will want to join. He is working on that airplane model they sent to him from England. We tiptoe past his door when we are at the Bennetts'. As soon as he is old enough, he'll be off to join the RAF.

Thursday, April 10, 1941

Tonight is our last choir practice before Easter. We are singing seriously now. Sam sounds great. Miss Little thinks he is a jewel. I heard her say so.

I have a new dress but it will be covered up by my choir gown most of the time. I feel special in that choir gown though, like somebody in a play, so I don't mind.

On Saturday we'll dye eggs. Pixie is coming over, and Robbie and Sam, of course. Last year I felt almost too old, but not this year. I am glad. I really like doing them. When I lift them out and they are a beautiful new colour, I feel as though I have worked a miracle.

Good Friday is tomorrow and our Easter holidays start. We won't have to go back to school for ten days. Lovely! Some families give their children Easter presents like watches or money. A lot get chocolate animals and candy eggs, but my parents say that is not what Easter is about.

They are right, I know, but I am glad we dye eggs and have new clothes for church.

Aunt Carrie and Grandpa will be coming home with us for dinner.

Good Friday morning, April 11, 1941

We are to sing in the Good Friday service this morning. We sing "Were You There?" And we join in the hymns.

The minister says Jesus could have chosen not to be crucified. I don't see how anyone could be so brave.

Bedtime

The service was beautiful, so sad. But I am too tired to write much tonight.

I'll just close by saying that Sam told me about a bombing raid our side made on Berlin. They hit the State Opera House. I wondered if that was like bombing Coventry Cathedral, but I kept quiet about it. There are some things that you can't say if you don't want to start a big argument.

Easter Sunday afternoon, April 13, 1941

Happy Easter, Diary.

We got up before dawn like the women in the Bible story and went to the sunrise service. We sang and it went well. The Senior Choir was not all there but Sam and I were.

Eleanor's hat looked especially beautiful. It has a veil that covers her face and does up under her chin with a velvet ribbon. It is fuchsia-coloured with a little lavender flower on the side. She looks ravishing in it. I wish we could send Bertie a coloured picture. He'd say she looks smashing.

Janie loves her hat, especially the yellow ribbon that dangles down her back and the three violets in a little bunch on the brim. Mine is white straw and simple but Mother says it looks lovely with my hair. And I won't be wearing it in the choir.

Christ is risen. Hallelujah!

Bedtime

It was a joyful day. George had sent us all cards he made. They are brilliant. Mother set them at our places at dinner. Mine has a bluebird of happiness flying to me with a rose in its beak. Grandpa said it was very fitting, since I do fly around and make everyone smile. He is a sweetie, as Jane says.

And so, dear Diary, Happy Easter to you.

Monday, April 14, 1941

Jane is busy cutting out the picture of Royal, the Saint Bernard dog that was presented to the king. He is the mascot of some troop. I hope they don't take the poor dog into battle. Jane is going to put his picture up on our wall. She wanted to put it next to my one of Peter Lawford. I made her start on her own wall. Royal is a handsome dog, but really!

You would think I would write more during these holidays, but I am too busy reading and celebrating spring and going for walks outdoors. Writing to George too, of course.

Tuesday, April 15, 1941

Today the boys and I were in the church with Mother, who was tidying away the Easter bouquets. She had gone downstairs for something, leaving us in the sanctuary. I was looking at the stained-glass windows when suddenly I got hit by a jet of water. I shrieked, of course. I could not believe it, but there stood Sam with Robbie's water pistol. He had loaded it with water from the FONT! Mother was not back, thank goodness. He got me on the side of my head so my clothes were not wet much. Anyway, Mother did not notice. Sam was shocked at himself. Robbie laughed so hard he rolled on the floor. It is a good thing Mother did not come back until we calmed down.

It is another good thing that Jane was over at Pixie's. She would have told on us for sure.

Thursday, April 17, 1941

That General Rommel who gave us trouble was pushed back at Tobruk by the British army. Dad says the African campaign is like a tug-of-war, first they win and then we do, back and forth. Sam says they are fighting in the desert. It must be torture to fight in such heat, and discouraging to win and then lose over and over.

Friday, April 18, 1941

Tonight the CGIT is going on a weekend camp. We will stay at Lake Bellwood and we won't be back until Sunday. I am leaving you at home, dear Diary. I don't want anyone reading you while my back is turned. We are going to have a marvellous time if we don't get too cold.

Tuesday, April 22, 1941

The camp was lots of fun but I was too tired and too busy to write about it yesterday, because exams are coming up soon. We learned new songs and laughed a lot. We also went walking in the woods near there, although it was muddy. Beth Fielding's boot got stuck in the mud and came off when I was hauling her out. We fell over laughing.

Wednesday, April 23, 1941

We have not had letters from the sailor boys. Dad reminded me that they are not on a pleasure cruise but fighting a war. If they do have spare time, they are probably in their bunks getting warm and catching up on missed sleep.

Sometimes letters get lost too and sometimes they come out of order.

Twenty-eight German prisoners of war escaped from the Lakehead. By now, they have all been captured. If they were still free, I would not be able to sleep because of imagining them coming in my bedroom window. I know, Diary. It's ridiculous to be afraid of that.

Dad said he felt sorry for them trying to get to the States from the Lakehead. The Americans have not come into the War yet so the Germans must have thought they would be safe there. Dad says the prison should give them geography lessons, because the distances between towns in Canada are far greater than in Europe. I wonder how those men feel being here.

Saturday, April 26, 1941

We are studying hard for exams. And I have a stack of new library books. I'll be back, Diary. But not for a day or two maybe.

Monday, April 28, 1941

I'm back!

We had to bring in a Current Event for school. I was already late so I grabbed the paper and cut out any old bit of war news that looked as though it would do. I got a bit about evacuating troops from Greece. There were 45,000 of them. I don't really understand the significance of it. Probably Sam will be able to explain. He is much better at following war news than I am. Thank goodness Miss McColl picked other people to read theirs out.

I'm really mostly interested in George's being safe. And his friend Bertie.

Wednesday, April 30, 1941

Sorry, but I am just not in a writing mood these days, Diary. I will soon recover. I must keep going until my birthday, as you know. Eleanor asks every so often.

MAY

May Day, Thursday, May 1, 1941

It is May Day. In British books, the children gather primroses and dance around maypoles and lovely things. But Jane says she never did any of those things. She knew about them from books too.

Friday, May 2, 1941

Frolicland was announced in tonight's paper. May 12 will be "Kiddie's Day." I hate being called a kiddie, but I like the rides and the cotton candy.

I have not had a letter from George for ages. None of us has. I try not to worry.

Saturday, May 3, 1941

Jane is becoming a good skipper and she can turn Double Dutch now. I remember when I used to have such trouble running in. I thought the rope might come down on me and cut me in two. Now it is SO simple.

Sunday, May 4, 1941

I am still not in a writing mood. George will have to wait and so will you, dear Diary. I wonder if Eleanor will examine every page and see when I skip or only write a line or two.

Tuesday, May 6, 1941

I almost put down that I had been busy writing to George, but it's not true. I was busy reading. I got into the What Katy Did series. The first one was the best.

Wednesday, May 7, 1941

George wrote, but he did not say much. He sounded tired. He said Bertie likes hearing from Eleanor. I was glad to hear I had not gone through all that anguish for nothing. She certainly likes the letters Bertie writes. This one from George was written two weeks ago and there have been none since for anybody.

Thursday, May 8, 1941

We have to write an essay for English called "Me, Myself and I." Well, that was the title I chose. Now I have to stop writing in you, dear Diary, and try to start the essay. The title sounded fine at first, but now my mind is a blank.

Friday, May 9, 1941

Sam came over before we finished breakfast. Jane was brushing her teeth, which was lucky because the war news was terrible! He had just heard a report on the radio. He could hardly get the words out. The Germans bombed London heavily again. Dad made Sam sit down before he went on and Mother went to keep Jane from coming downstairs for a few minutes. The House of Commons and the British Museum and Westminster Abbey were all damaged.

Dad turned on the radio and it was true. Those famous places were not demolished, but they have holes in their roofs. Sam started to tell us about going to the Museum with his class and he started to cry. I don't think he is only minding about the famous places. He is wild with worry about his family.

Jane finished her teeth and then heard his voice and came running. Dad told her the news but toned it down. She was not fooled. She ran and flung her arms around Sam and he hugged her. I almost cried.

Nobody knew what to do next. We just sat there looking sick. Then Jane stood up and astonished everyone by saying we should go to school or we'd be late. I looked at her and thought about her father saying they were the bravest of the brave. He was right. It is strange. We know bombs are falling on London night after night, but it stops seeming real. Then actual places are named and suddenly it is not unreal any longer.

Saturday, May 10, 1941

We went to the movies this afternoon. I cried, but not really because the movie was so sad. I think sadness builds up deep inside us and then some little thing opens a door and lets it rush out. It is not a particular sadness but all the bits rolled into a ball of tears.

Sunday, May 11, 1941

Today was Mother's Day. We would have brought her breakfast in bed but she hates crumbs in her covers, she said. We did set the table before she came down and she sat at her place and let us wait on her. Jane poached her an egg and she had to use her knife to hack a bite off it. Jane watched her chewing and said, "I guess I cooked it a little too long."

"It is delicious," said my noble mother.

Lizby gave a little snort.

We put our money together and bought her spring flowers. She loved them.

We all wore flowers pinned on our coats when we

went to church. I had a red tulip because Mother is alive. She wore a white one because her mother is dead. They don't do it that way in England, Jane says.

Monday, May 12, 1941

Today we all went to Frolicland and rode on The Octopus. It was exciting until Robbie turned green and started to be sick. I screamed at them to stop and they did! He got off and threw up right away. They made us all get off and leave. I thought that was unfair. Sam said what Robbie did was a bad advertisement for the ride. Then we got laughing. Robbie only managed a weak smile though.

Thank goodness there was a merry-go-round. Jane and Pixie rode it three times and would have gone again if we had given them more money. But every ride cost 5¢.

Jane called the cotton candy "candy floss." I don't know why I like it so much. It does not taste like anything else.

Tuesday, May 13, 1941

Last Saturday, a man called Rudolph Hess parachuted into Scotland and gave himself up to the British. He was a great friend of Hitler's. Nobody understands it. He put his hands up and said, "No bombs on my plane!" Dad says it is astonishing and he is as fascinated as though R.H. were a famous villain. He was lucky not to get shot when he landed like that.

We wanted to go to the show tonight but Mother and Dad said no. They went without us and came home laughing. The movie had Jimmy Stewart and Hedy Lamarr in it. I told Eleanor I thought I was old enough to go and she said Mother and Dad hardly ever get out by themselves and I should think about that. After all, we had been to Frolicland yesterday.

I hate it when I am in the wrong that way.

Last year I would have made a big fuss. Maybe I am growing more mature just the way Eleanor said I would. I would like to believe this but I don't think it is likely.

Still no letter from George, or Bertie either.

Thursday, May 15, 1941

Boring day. No mail from G or B. If something bad had happened to them, the government would have sent word, wouldn't they, Diary?

Friday, May 16, 1941

Today Barbara told me that her family got news that the Nazis had arrested thousands of Jews in Paris.

I did not know what to say. It sounds crazy. Wicked too, but also senseless. I know the Steiners have relatives in France. Barbara showed me a picture of two of her cousins once. They looked so small and sweet. Where would the Nazis put so many prisoners? It makes no sense. Do they arrest them just because they are Jews? Why? I can't understand any of it.

Eleanor is starting to study harder. She will be trying for her Senior Matriculation in June. She'll have to write nine Departmental exams. They are sent away to be marked by strangers. Your name is not on them, just a number. Being an egghead, Eleanor will pass with flying colours.

Saturday, May 17, 1941

Thirty-five enemy soldiers surrendered to our troops in Ethiopia. Do you suppose they will be sent to Ontario like those other prisoners of war? We are a very long way away from Ethiopia. I looked it up in the atlas. We have cold winters, especially up at the Lakehead. Ethiopia must be hot.

Everyone in the family is worried because we have not heard from George. I told them about Barbara's cousin Daniel going on a mission and coming back safe and sound and that was a little comfort. But not much.

Sunday, May 18, 1941

Barbara was right to be afraid for the Jewish people. Her family is terribly upset by the news from France. They are still trying to get people out.

I asked her if she wanted to come over for a while but she said she had to go home and be with her mother.

Monday, May 19, 1941

I was positive we would get mail today, but none came. Soon it will be my birthday. If George can write to me then, I am sure he will. I will write to him again right now.

Tuesday, May 20, 1941

I have too much homework, Diary. I'll get back to you when I catch up. I will not forget you. After all, I've written in you for close to a year.

Thursday, May 22, 1941

The Steiners heard that yesterday the Nazis forbade any emigration of Jews from France. What does it mean? Why don't they just let them leave France if they want to?

No mail from G.

Friday, May 23, 1941

George is missing. I can't

Later

I must write it down. We got a telegram. George's ship was torpedoed, but the telegram did not say when. There must have been some survivors. Maybe a lifeboat is missing. If not, the telegram would have said George was lost, wouldn't it? That is what I keep telling myself.

We want to get in touch with Bertie's family and see if they have heard anything more. Is Bertie missing too? But we do not know his home address.

Oh, dear Diary, what has happened to them?

Bedtime

Books say mothers will know if their sons are alive. I can't ask though. Mother looks so white and sick.

Saturday, May 24, 1941

Victoria Day

It is Queen Victoria's birthday and it would be a holiday if it were a school day. But I cannot write about anything happy. Mother looks pale as a ghost and I don't think she has slept at all since we heard. Dad's face is stiff with holding in his feelings, I guess.

Pixie came dashing in to show us her new hair ribbons and I had to smile at her. But underneath, there was just a freezing cold emptiness inside me. I've never felt anything like this before. I am glad to go to bed because you can get away from the fear while you sleep.

I remember how terrible it was when the *City of Benares* was sunk and when Coventry was bombed. But they were like sad stories that made you cry. George being missing is not just a story. George is my brother who woke me up at six o'clock on my birthday phoning long distance.

I can't help crying, but the tears are not just sad ones. They hurt. They blot the page. And they don't help the pain go away.

Sunday, May 25, 1941

Afternoon

I can hardly bear to look into Mother's face. Or Dad's.

Lizby comes into the kitchen in the morning with red eyes. And Grandpa keeps saying we must not worry because he is praying for George's safety. But his voice shakes and you can hear how afraid he is.

I am praying too, Grandpa.

And I am afraid.

Evening

The war news makes it worse. The *Bismarck* sank the British ship *Hood*. 1416 crew members are lost. Did they tell the sailors' families they were missing or that they died?

Mother and Eleanor went to church. I couldn't. I took Jane to Sunday School. I sat there in a sort of blur. They were talking about the lost lamb and how the shepherd searched for it. I like that story but it was hard to bear today. I was glad to get away. On the way home, Jane held my hand.

Monday, May 26, 1941

No news. Oh, Diary, it is so hard to bear.

Tuesday, May 27, 1941

Sam got a letter from Terry. He is still fine even though his family has moved away from the street they used to live on. He said their house was smashed to rubble the night before they left, but they were safe in the Anderson shelter their neighbours dug. Sam was reading the letter out loud because Terry's writing is hard to decipher. He also said they have had a letter from Alan delivered by the Red Cross.

Sam came to the end and just sat staring at the floor. We all knew he was thinking of George. He feels it as though George is his brother too. He tried to say something and then just left without speaking.

Oh, where is my brother? Is Bertie with him?

Please, God, keep them safe.

Wednesday, May 28, 1941

They sank the *Bismarck!*

More dead sailors, even if they are Germans. I can't write about it. I keep picturing them in the water struggling to stay alive.

Thursday, May 29, 1941

George is alive! George is alive!

I have to write it again. It won't stay shut in my head. George is alive!

That was all the cable said. A letter will follow. It did not mention Bertie. We have so many questions.

But my brother is ALIVE!

Saturday, May 31, 1941

Mother and Dad are overjoyed that George is alive, and they're frantic with worry, yet they both go right on with their usual lives. I don't see how they can. Yet we will go to school, which is sort of the same. I don't think I will learn anything. Miss McColl is kind and never asks to see my homework. Thank goodness the weekend has come.

I wish I could write in tall golden letters that danced up and down on the page

George

is

alive!

Later

No more news yet. No mail on Sunday, of course. Why can't they tell us more?

JUNE

Sunday, June 1, 1941

Mother said we should write to George even though we have not heard any more news. He will be waiting for word of home. So we had a letter-writing binge. Jane wrote, and Lizby. Then Aunt Carrie came by and she sat down and added a note too. George is going to be deluged with news from home.

Monday, June 2, 1941

At last, we got a short airmail letter telling us about George. Someone from the hospital wrote. He and his friends were in a lifeboat and then drifted ashore. This happened about two weeks ago. But we still don't know how they are. The letter said he was as well as could be expected.

I did not know anyone would really say that. It answers none of our million questions. Is he wounded? Will he be all right?

Tuesday, June 3, 1940

We finally heard from George himself. He wrote a line and then dictated the rest to a nurse. He was in that lifeboat for two days! Bertie and four other men were with him. Bertie is alive. George's left hand was crushed. He says his fingers look like huge bruised sausages. They put leeches on them to suck out the dead blood! He sent his love and will write again.

The person who wrote the words for him said he is doing well. His friend however had a head wound and is still unconscious. She must mean Bertie.

I thought I would throw up when he told about the leeches.

Wednesday, June 4, 1940

Nothing seems real. We are waiting for news from England. Nothing today.

Thursday, June 5, 1941

We got a longer letter written just the day after. It tells about Bertie. He is in the same hospital as George but in a different wing. He is still very ill. He got a bad head wound. He was struck on the head by wreckage. They hauled him to safety and wrapped his head in strips of cloth they tore off clothes.

The nurses wheeled George to visit Bertie. He has not spoken but George is sure he can see and hear.

Later

I was inspired and told Eleanor to post off her best picture right away and she kissed me and ran to get one. It was the new one with her Easter hat and, with it, an old one of her sitting on our front steps looking not so glamorous. Eleanor is wise sometimes. It would be far more comforting to a sick sailor.

But our George is alive!!!!! That is the marvellous thing.

Friday, June 6, 1941

No more letters this afternoon, but we sent a package of candy and cookies. Aunt Carrie put in a box of Laura Secords, every one of them chewy. They are George's favourites. I like the buttercreams better myself.

In all the excitement about George I forgot to mention that Mother bought me a reversible coat for $5.95. It is an early birthday present. I love it and she says it was a real bargain. It is brown on one side and green on the other. I call it my celebration coat.

There was a parade with six bands on June 1st. It was to get people to buy Victory Bonds. Dad did, although I don't know how much. I didn't write about it because we did not go.

There's a bigger parade coming up and Jane is going to march with her class. It is called a Torch Parade.

I keep sending prayers and good wishes to George and Bertie and writing to tell them about all the goings-on here. I hope it cheers them up.

Later

I was telling about the Torch Parade. It means the torch in the Flanders Fields poem by Colonel John McCrae. It says:

Take up our quarrel with the foe:
To you from failing hands we throw
The torch; be yours to hold it high.

I think it means that you have to keep fighting for the dead soldiers even though they are gone. I like the earlier part better about the larks who keep singing even though they can't be heard because of the thundering of the guns.

There are to be four thousand children in the parade! It will end up at the McCrae House. Dad took me to see that house when I was ten. Is the house part of history? I am not sure about houses. If they have bullet holes in the walls or King Charles slept in them, then they are history, but what if everyday people just lived ordinary lives in them?

George is part of history though, and Daniel and Bertie and Terry's brother and all the rest.

Saturday, June 7, 1941

Jane is outside with Pixie, bouncing a ball against the side of the house. I just heard her chant,

I'm a little Dutch girl dressed in blue.
Here are some things I like to do.
Salute the Captain. Bow to the Queen.
Turn my back on the dirty submarine.
Fly a spitfire to Paris, France,
And give Mr. Hitler a kick in the pants!

I knew the first part, but I never heard the line about Mr. Hitler getting a kick in the pants. I think they keep making up new words.

Sunday, June 8, 1941

Yesterday we got a letter from a friend of George's who was on leave when the ship was sunk. He told us there were two dead men in the boat by the time it reached shore. George did not tell us that, but Dad says not to keep asking George to tell us more. He will need time. "Wounds to the spirit like George's will last long after his body is healed," he said.

I never heard of this before.

In church, Dr. Gallegher thanked God for George's deliverance. It made me feel queer thinking about all the others that died.

Monday, June 9, 1941

We got another letter. George told us that Bertie holds Eleanor's picture up and smiles. He has not spoken yet. His head is still bandaged but not his face. He thinks he saw Bertie kiss the picture but he was not sure. Eleanor blushed and ran out of the room. But she has the letter upstairs.

I wonder when her new photo will reach him.

Tuesday, June 10, 1941

George's letter also gave us the name of another man who never gets mail because his wife and baby died in the Blitz, so we are writing to him too. It is hard to do but I try to pretend he is just like George.

School keeps going all the time. My birthday is one week away. I actually managed to keep my promise and write in you for twelve months!

Wednesday, June 11, 1941

AMAZING NEWS! Prepare yourself, Diary.

Mr. and Mrs. Browning came to visit George in hospital. And Mrs. Browning is EXPECTING A BABY!!! Jane is going to be a big sister! Sam too, of course. A big brother, I mean. Everyone is flabbergasted. He — or she — is due any day.

The Brownings did not tell Sam and Jane because they didn't want to upset them and they decided to wait until the baby arrived. But George told them he was sure the kids would be pleased as punch and he was going to "let the cat out of the bag."

When Dad read that bit, he said that was an unfortunate choice of words on George's part, as though Mrs. Browning is a bag.

Anyway, Jane and Sam are excited and happy mostly, although it does make them want to go home badly.

Thursday, June 12, 1941

We talk about the baby, all the time.

Jane is looking in our *A Name for Baby* book. She says she will choose. After Britty and Only, I am not sure this is such a great idea.

Maybe the baby will be born on my birthday! Now that would be great.

Friday, June 13, 1941

Eleanor got a letter from Bertie's mother! She wrote to thank her for her kindness in writing to Bertie. Eleanor was so surprised and pleased. Bertie's family comes from Sussex, which is where some of our ancestors lived. She sent a picture of them. He has three little sisters. His father is a postman. Eleanor wrote right back but she had trouble thinking up what to say. I helped.

It was a lovely thing to happen on Friday the 13th, which is supposed to be unlucky.

Saturday, June 14, 1941

The kitten got lost today. We spent all day mopping up Jane's tears and searching. He had been asleep, shut up in Jane's dresser drawer. At suppertime he woke up and began to yowl. It was almost like getting the news that George was alive!

Sunday, June 15, 1941

No exciting news today. My birthday is nearly here. So is the baby's. As I have already told you, I hate waiting.

Monday, June 16, 1941

Thank goodness I have a new library book to read tonight. I can't stand the minutes crawling by so S L O W L Y! I am taking my book to bed.

Tuesday, June 17, 1941

Happy Birthday to Charlotte Mary Twiss! I am now thirteen!

Barbara's mother actually let her come over to my birthday supper this year! And Barbara was lovely to Jane and Sam. Maybe she is maturing too.

I got my reward from Eleanor. I got two. The first was another diary. She laughed when she gave it to me and pretended that it was the big prize. A year ago, I might have been fooled, but I know her better now. So much has happened in our lives during my thirteenth year, just as she said it would.

The other reward, the big surprise, is that she has planned a whole day in Toronto with me. The two of us are to go down in the train and have lunch at Eaton's and go to a matinee and visit Britnell's. It is a famous bookstore, one filled with just books. Here, the book-stores sell stationery and games and jigsaws. She will buy me whatever book I choose. We will not come home until after supper. It sounds so grown-up!

But did I myself change in this past year? Eleanor said I would. I thought at first that I had not, but I read the whole diary over to see, and I am different. I can't explain exactly how.

But I understand things I missed when I was just beginning this year. Part of it is because of all the sadness which has come to us. Missing George, and the bombs, and the sinking of the *City of Benares*, and the War going on and on.

I remember that I used to be sad mostly for myself, but I think I know now how it feels to hurt for other people. I was so frightened about George and worried over Bertie. And I think more about how other people feel, like Jane and the rest.

I am taller, of course, and my body is changing. But that is private.

And I have maybe learned how to be a good big sister.

Now to begin the fourteenth year in the life of Charlotte Mary Twiss!

The End

P.S.

Wednesday, June 18, 1941

The cable, to Sam and Jane both, came at breakfast time.

Jane was so good. She waited until we got Sam before she let us open it. It was their Baby, of course. it

said, WILLIAM CHARLES BORN AT TWO THIS MORN-
ING STOP SEVEN POUNDS STOP MOTHER AND
CHILD FINE STOP LOVE DAD.

Sam cheered but Jane looked as though she was not
sure whether to laugh or cry.

"If only he had come yesterday," she said. "Then he
would have been born on Charlotte's birthday."

Then my clever father told her that he WAS born on
my birthday, because at 2 a.m. in England, here it was
still YESTERDAY. Clever Dad. Well done, William!

See you in Volume Two, dear Diary. Now I am a
teenager. Who knows what will happen next.

EPILOGUE

While people are involved in fighting a war, it seems that once peace is declared, the world will not only return to normal, but be filled with joy and laughter. The Twiss family and the Browning children certainly celebrated on VE (Victory in Europe) Day in May 1945, when the war in Europe ended, and on VJ (Victory over Japan) Day in August 1945, when Japan surrendered. But when the cheering stopped, it was time for Sam and Jane and Pixie to go home to England.

Sam and Charlotte were about to begin their second-last year in high school. Jane was thirteen and had finished Grade Nine. Pixie, who was only five when she left home, was ten, and barely remembered her British family. Everyone was pulled in two directions, longing to go and wanting to stay.

Once he reached home, Sam completed the courses he needed to enable him to return to Guelph to attend the Ontario Veterinary College and become a veterinarian. After graduating, he went back home to Britain to treat large animals, among which were the work horses he had grown to love as a boy. He also took flying lessons and joined with some friends in buying a small plane.

Jane missed Charlotte and the rest of the Twiss family, but was comforted by Skip's obvious delight at her return. She also loved being a big sister to her new brother Will, who thought she was wonderful. When Jane grew up, she became a children's librarian and collected dogs in need of a loving home. She often brought one with her to work, which delighted the boys and girls who counted on her to find them just the right book.

Pixie fought to stay in Canada but finally had to go home. She remained miserable until she visited the Brownings in England and discovered she had not left all her new friends on the other side of the Atlantic. She married when she was nineteen and had a large family. Luckily, she lived close to Jane, who was a great help in raising Pixie's boisterous youngsters.

When George came home to Canada after the war, he brought a young Scottish wife with him. They lived in Toronto, where he got a job working for a newspaper. Eventually he made a name for himself as a cartoonist and illustrator.

Bertie's injuries were too severe for him to live a normal life after the war. He spent close to three years in a convalescent hospital in England, and then was sent home, where he lived for the rest of his life.

Eleanor grieved for him and sympathized with his situation even more when, in 1947 while working for her masters degree in social work, she contracted polio. She recovered slowly, but never regained full use of her left side. After months of treatment, she grew able to walk again, although she had to wear a leg brace and use a cane for balance.

When Charlotte was allowed to visit her sister in hospital, she grew interested in helping with Eleanor's physiotherapy. She ended up becoming a qualified occupational and physiotherapist in Toronto, working with disabled children.

At that time, it was difficult for a woman with a disability like Eleanor's to find a fulfilling job. Finally she began to tutor high school students who were in danger of failing, and she did so well at it that she soon had a waiting list of pupils. She continued to live at home but, through the church and her pupils' families, she made many good friends and had an active social life. When she and a friend visited England one summer, Sam took her for a ride in his plane.

After Mrs. Twiss died, Charlotte realized that both her sister and her father needed her help, so she came home to live. At thirty-four, she surprised all her friends and relatives, except her father, by marrying his doctor. Two years later she give birth to a baby boy whom she called Charles after her father and Richard after her husband.

Although everyone but Bertie seemed to flourish after the war ended, each of them was left with scars. The tug-of-war had given them an uncertainty about the future, and a fear of what calamity might beset them next. The memory of Bertie's suffering remained with both George and Charlotte, and Eleanor's illness made them aware that even in peacetime, heartache is never far away.

Yet joy was there too. Whenever two or more of them came together, the memories of what Charlotte called the War Guest Years were brought out and laughed over and Charlotte's diary was often consulted and enjoyed.

"You know what, Charlotte? You weren't the only one who matured that year," Sam said on one visit. "We all did."

And it was true.

HISTORICAL NOTE

Charlotte Twiss, the main character in this book, begins her journal ten months after the outbreak of World War II and ends it a year later. It is not until six months after her journal ends that the Japanese bombed Pearl Harbor, bringing the Americans into the war. The worldwide conflict went on for three and a half years after that.

Before Canada declared war on Germany in September 1939, Germany had invaded Austria and taken over much of Czechoslovakia. When the Germans marched into Poland and swiftly conquered it, the British, who had struggled to negotiate a binding peace treaty with Hitler, finally declared war. Canada followed suit a week later. This delay was because our prime minister wanted to show that Canada was no longer merely a British colony, but an independent nation.

The following spring, Denmark, Norway, Holland and Belgium fell before Hitler's troops. In late May–early June 1940 the British could not hold out against the German advance and were forced to retreat to France's west coast at Dunkirk. Thousands of British soldiers were trapped on the beach and would have been massacred but for hundreds of British civilians who sailed across the English Channel time after time to rescue them. While three hundred thousand Allied soldiers were ferried to safety by the Navy ships and the civilian boats, the RAF kept up a covering fire to hold the Germans at bay. Although many thousands were saved, thousands of others, both soldiers and rescuers, were killed. Very shortly after the men were rescued from the beaches at Dunkirk, France was occupied by German troops and forced to surrender.

During 1939, British families had begun to send a few children overseas to ensure their safety. As the English heard news of German tanks, backed by highly trained troops, overrunning and defeating one country after another, they were thankful that the English Channel separated them from the rest of Europe. Yet this age-old barrier to invasion was no longer the defence it had once been. Soon, Britons were sure, German planes would target English cities for bombing raids. Hundreds of thousands of children were evacuated to rural areas. The government arranged for those who had no families in remote British villages to place their children in the homes of strangers.

Thousands of parents even chose to send their boys and girls halfway around the world to keep them safe. After all, in May of 1940 the Germans had launched their *blitzkrieg* ("lightning war") on Holland, Luxembourg, Belgium and France. In August 1940 the German Luftwaffe began attacks on Royal Air Force radar stations and airfields. It was clear to all that British cities such as Plymouth, Coventry, Bristol, Liverpool and London would be slated for air raids.

No bombs fell at first. During August and early September 1940, the German Luftwaffe and the RAF battled in the skies above England and the English Channel. This was known as the Battle of Britain. Both sides suffered heavy losses of planes and pilots.

Then the German command shifted to bombing British cities, partly hoping to destroy the war effort, partly to try to break down the staunch morale of the British people. On September 7, 1940, wave after wave of German planes filled the skies over London, pounding the city with thousands of bombs. Fires set off by the first attack lit the way for the swarm of planes that followed. The deafening noise struck terror into the bravest hearts. The Blitz had begun, and for the next fifty-seven days bombs kept raining down on London. Houses toppled, fires raged and people were buried in rubble. Of the forty thousand people in Britain who died in the Blitz, over half were in London itself.

Before these bombing raids actually began, children had been issued with gas masks. During air raids, sirens would sound, alerting city dwellers that approaching aircraft had been sighted. People would hurry to places of safety. Some took refuge in homemade air-raid shelters they had dug in their back gardens. Others headed for the nearest Underground station. (Canadians call this the subway.)

The children who had been sent away to safe havens agonized as the radio broadcasts and newspapers told the harrowing story. *They* were safe . . . but what was happening to their parents?

Many of these evacuees have told about their experiences during WWII and the Blitz. Several good novels about those times have also been written. *Goodnight, Mr. Tom* by Michele Magorian is one of the best of these. It is the story of a small sad boy who is taken to live with an old man who does not want a child foisted on him. The story of how both of them are changed as they learn to love each other is great, but the book also shows what happened to a village when a bunch of children from London descend upon it. *Carrie's War* by Nina Bawden is based upon the writer's own experiences when she and her brother were sent to live in a village in Wales.

Many girls and boys were placed in settings completely unlike those they had always known. The host families also had a difficult time struggling to understand this influx of unhappy youngsters. For some it was an enriching and ultimately happy experience. For others it was a bitter struggle. They differed in so many ways — how they spoke, the food they ate, the games they played, their way of settling quarrels, their ideas about courage, their manners. Many felt fiercely loyal to their own families too, and saw any request to alter their behaviour as an attack on their home values.

It was not easy for the host families in Britain either, with many men away fighting, and with such an influx of newcomers causing overcrowding in schools and straining already-stressed resources as the country continued to wage war.

But at least the children evacuated within Britain knew that they were still in the same land as their own families. Although phoning home was not taken for granted in those days, and not everyone had a phone, it was possible to stay in touch to some extent via letters, postcards and even occasional visits.

War guests like Sam and Jane had all of the problems faced by those evacuees, made worse by being shipped across a great ocean. The trip itself was dangerous, and some children returned to England after the ship they were on was badly damaged by a German attack.

Although some of the evacuees who reached Canada had been sent to live with relatives, or were kept together with others from their private schools, many children were taken in by Canadian families whose hearts had been touched by their plight, but whom the war guests did not even know. Kit Pearson, in her Guests of War trilogy beginning with *The Sky Is Falling*, vividly recounts the experiences of two such fictional children.

Most of the war guests in Canada came in 1940. Some "private" evacuees were sent to live with relatives in Canada, or to stay at a private schools such as

Toronto's Bishop Strachan School and Branksome Hall. Several thousand were sent by Britain's Children's Overseas Reception Board (CORB), a government agency set up to handle the evacuee situation.

Although there is no sure tally of the total number of children who came to Canada, they definitely numbered in the thousands. Thousands more children were expected, but on September 17, 1940, a large ship packed with war guest children, the *City of Benares*, was torpedoed and sunk. Seventy-seven children and over half the crew were killed. Panicked parents in England realized that in trying to send their children to safety, they might be sending them to their death. Most withdrew their children from the evacuee program, and even though some still wished to send their children overseas, the British government sent no further children to Canada.

Thousands of boys and girls were already here by then, and here most of them stayed for five years, until the war was over. Some war guests initially had difficulties fitting in, and even had to be moved to different host families. But on the whole they grew to feel they belonged. They were spared some of the problems faced by evacuees who remained in Britain — they were not so close to home and they did not expect Canadian adults to behave as their parents would, so the differences actually made the transition easier for some of them. They *had* to adjust. Besides, they could not easily plan to run away, not with an ocean between them and their families.

Some of the war guests were so young that they had no understanding of the length of time they might be away. When they had been in Canada for three or four years, many found writing letters home difficult. How could they keep their love alive when the people to whom they were supposed to write had become, in some instances, distant strangers? They had grown close to the people who had given them a home in Canada, often coming to consider these their parents, and their own parents more like aunts and uncles.

When the war ended and the war guests could return to their homes in Britain, it was exciting for some and terribly hard for others. Some also had to face the scorn felt for them by children who had spent the war years in England — although the war guests did not come to Canada of their own choice but because their parents had sent them, some children in Britain called them cowards for running away when their country was in trouble. The evacuees had not suffered the severe food rationing, the blackouts, the bombing raids or the fear experienced by those who stayed behind, either. It often took some time for the returning children to readjust and find their feet again. Some managed this; others never felt quite "at home" again.

Throughout Charlotte's diary, her friend Barbara Steiner tells of her anxiety about her Jewish relatives in

Europe. The Steiners tried to get them out of danger, but could not. The Nazis' systematic persecution of Jews began when the party was formed in 1920. This escalated until it ended in the Holocaust, when six million Jews were killed. Unless they themselves were Jewish, Canadian children were largely unaware of this situation until the Allied troops that liberated the concentration camps discovered the gas chambers and the mass graves, as well as the remaining prisoners, who had been starved until they resembled skeletons. Though Canadian Jews tried to get Jewish children in Europe out of danger, only a handful were rescued.

As I did research for this story, I discovered that many war guests later emigrated to the countries which had taken them in: Australia, the United States or Canada. Many Canadian children today are descended from someone who once was a lonesome war guest. Those ancestors would never have thought that they would settle in this strange and frightening land, a land that eventually become their heart's home.

British Expressions and What They Mean

bisbuit: cookie
candy floss: cotton candy
dinner: lunch
frock: dress
ha'penny: coin worth half a British penny
headmaster: principal
ice lolly: popsicle
jersey: a long-sleeved pullover shirt
joint: roast
jumper: pullover sweater
knickers: girls' underpants
the loo: the toilet
lorry: truck
mackintosh or mack: raincoat
maize: corn
to paddle: to wade
Patience: Solitaire
plaster or sticking plaster: bandage
plimsolls: running shoes
pudding: any dessert
shilling: British coin worth 12 pence
tea: late afternoon meal (like North American supper)
torch: flashlight
treacle: syrup
tuppence: British coin worth 2 pence
vest: undershirt
wellies or Wellingtons: rubber boots

A list of clothing that government-sponsored children were required to take with them:

Boys:

2 vests
2 pairs of underpants
pair of trousers
2 pairs of socks
6 handkerchiefs
pullover or jersey

Girls:

vest
pair of knickers
petticoat
2 pairs of stockings
6 handkerchiefs
slip
blouse
cardigan

What else did they pack in their suitcases?

overcoat or mackintosh
comb
1 pair of Wellington boots
towel
soap
facecloth
toothbrush
boots or shoes
plimsolls
sandwiches
packet of nuts and raisins
dry biscuits
barley sugar (rather than sugar)
apple

Tearful children sit before the rubble that was once their home in London, September 1940.

A girl in Battersea (right) stands in front of her ruined home following a bombing raid.
(Below) Children evacuate London by train, en route to a safer location in the British countryside. They could not know that it might be five years before they were able to return home.

*A group of British children huddled in a ditch look up when
they hear bombers flying overhead during an air raid in 1940.*

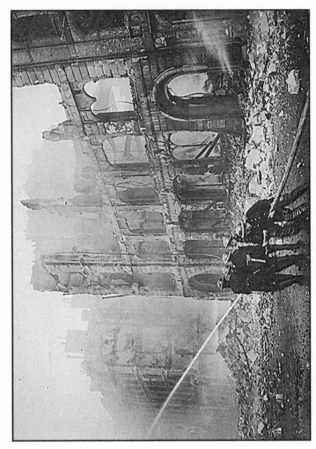

Firefighters in London struggle to put out a fire after one of the nightly raids, this one in 1941.

Daily life in bombed British towns and cities still carried on despite fear and upheaval. Schooling was often disrupted because of air raids, or because students had spent the night in an air-raid shelter.

Evacuee children from Britain arrive in Montreal, Quebec, July 7, 1940. Most had no idea they would be staying until the war ended in 1945.

Sailors recently enlisted in the Royal Canadian Navy depart Ottawa's Union Station in November, 1940.

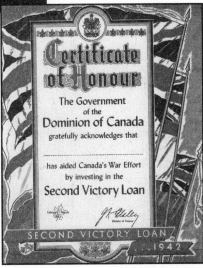

(Left) The Canadian government created many posters urging citizens to purchase victory bonds. (Below) Certificates were given to Canadians who took out loans in order to buy Victory Bonds in support of the war effort.

On the home front, posters such as this one (right) urged children to collect rags, old metal, scrap paper — even milkweed pods for stuffing lifejackets — as part of the war effort.

(Below) A boys' group poses with collected scrap metal.

Princesses Elizabeth (right) and Margaret Rose speak to evacuee children on the BBC in October 1940, a month after the Blitz began.

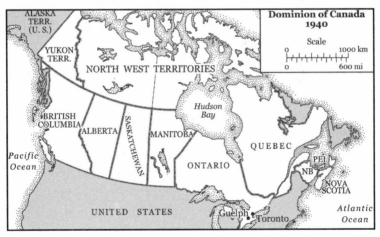

Canada in 1940. At that time Newfoundland and Labrador were still not part of the country.

ACKNOWLEDGMENTS

Grateful acknowledgment is made for permission to reprint the following:

Cover portrait: Christine Cann, courtesy of Steve Cann.
Cover background: *Bristol at war 1941*, courtesy of Paul Townsend.

Page 206: from John McCrae's "In Flanders Fields".
Page 227: Courtesy of Mandy Barrow.
Page 228: National Archives and Records Administration, NA-306-NT-3163V.
Page 229 (upper): Toni Frissell, Library of Congress, LC-F9-02-4501-24A.
Page 229 (lower): *London's Children*, Parker/Hulton Archive/Getty Images, 3070717.
Page 230: Library of Congress, LC-USZ62-93161.
Page 231: National Archives and Records Administration, 306-NT-901C(11).
Page 232: National Archives and Records Administration, 195566.
Page 233: *The third contingent of evacuee children from Britain*, Library and Archives Canada, PA-142400.
Page 234: *Unidentified members of the Royal Canadian Navy in a train leaving Union Station, Ottawa, Ontario, November, 1940*, Library and Archives Canada, PA-204286.
Page 235 (upper): *Buy Victory Bonds*, Archives of Ontario, C 232-2-12-0-2.
Page 235 (lower): *Certificate of Honour, Second Victory Loan*, William Ready Division of Archives and Research Collections, McMaster University Library, 00001109.
Page 236 (upper): *We Want Rags for Vital War Needs!*, Library and Archives Canada, C-087546.
Page 237 (lower): *Boys' group does salvage work*, The *Gazette* Photo Collection/Library and Archives Canada, PA-108279.
Page 237 (upper): *Royal broadcast*, Topical Press Agency/Hulton Archive/Getty Images, 3425153.
Page 239 (lower): Map by Paul Heersink/Paperglyphs. Map data © 1999 Government of Canada with permission from Natural Resources Canada.

238

This story is for Charlotte Mary Langridge
Born January 15, 2008.
Tuesday's child is full of grace.
And for Madison, Sidney, Natalie and Azlin.

The publisher wishes to thank Dr. Helen Brown of Vancouver Island University, author of "Negotiating Space, Time, and Identity: The Hutton-Pellett Letters and a British Child's Wartime Evacuation to Canada," published in *Letters Across Borders: The Epistolary Practices of International Migrants*, for sharing her expertise. Thanks also to Barbara Hehner for her careful checking of the factual details.

ABOUT THE AUTHOR

When Jean Little's family came home from Taiwan to live in Canada in August, 1939, Jean was seven years old. The Littles landed just one month before the outbreak of World War II. She was eight when British children, known as war guests, began to be sent from England to safety in Canada. In the summer of 1940, Jane Browning and Jean Little were the same age and for both, Canada was an unknown country.

Although she was younger than Charlotte, Jean was able to draw on many childhood memories for this story. She knew three children who were war guests. She remembers giving half her allowance to buy War Savings Stamps. She saw Hitler and his goose-stepping troops in newsreels. She also saw movies featuring child actress Elizabeth Taylor, who was just one month younger than she was. How excited everyone was when the first movies in colour were shown!

Jean longed for a rubber doll which you could bathe, but nothing made of rubber was available because it was needed for the war effort. Plastic had not been invented, so broken dolls were common. And no rubber meant no elastic. Women did up their underpants with a button and there were lots of stories about these buttons coming undone and the pants dropping to the ground in church or downtown.

When Jean and her brothers were kids, they listened to favourite radio programs on their big family radio, just as children today watch TV shows. She also knows what it's like when your parents take in children who need a home — something her own mother did, just like Mrs. Twiss taking in Jane, but also giving Sam and Pixie and even Terry a home when they needed one. Like Charlotte, Jean had mixed feelings about having to share.

One of Jean's favourite parts of working on this story was remembering the words to old songs until she could sing them right through again. She also enjoyed listening, on Talking Book, to Kit Pearson's The Guests of War trilogy, plus most of the other stories that the children in the book enjoy. One of the hard parts about recalling the past, she says, is wanting to put every vivid memory into your book but facing the sad fact that you can't.

Jean Little is one of Canada's — and the world's — best-loved writers for children. She has published almost fifty books, including novels, autobiographies, poetry and picture books. Some of her best-known titles include *From Anna*; *Mine for Keeps*; *Willow and Twig*, *Hey World, Here I Am*; *One to Grow On*; *Once Upon a Golden Apple* and *Little by Little*. Jean is the author of three prior books in the Dear Canada series: CLA Book of the Year Award winner *Orphan at My Door*, CLA Honour Book *Brothers Far from Home* and Red Cedar nominee *If I Die Before I Wake*. Her recent novel *Dancing Through the Snow*, about an abandoned girl helping a dog rescued from a puppy mill, was short-listed for the Ruth and Sylvia Schwartz Award and the

Diamond Willow Award. *Pippin the Christmas Pig* won the Mr. Christie Book Award, and *Listen, Said the Donkey* was a Canadian Children's Book Centre starred selection. Jean's most recent picture book, *The Sweetest One of All,* was named a Toronto Public Library First and Best Book. Among her many other awards are the Vicky Metcalf Award for Body of Work and the Order of Canada. Jean has been nominated four times for the prestigious Astrid Lindgren Memorial Award.

Jean lives in Guelph, Ontario, with her sister Pat, her great niece and nephew, two cats and four dogs, including her guide dog Honey.

ACKNOWLEDGMENTS

I have so many people to thank for help with this book that I am sure I am going to leave someone out, but I am deeply grateful to those I name below and to anyone I might omit.

First of all, my thanks go to Sandy Bogart Johnston, the editor of the Dear Canada series. Her patience, humour, insight and editing skills are phenomenal. I am also grateful to Diane Kerner, who read Charlotte's diary with intelligence and enjoyment. Thank you, too, to all at Scholastic who work hard to make this series so appealing.

My sister, Pat de Vries, not only helped with research but often came to my rescue when I was stuck or grew discouraged. My niece, Robin Little, found me song lyrics, movie titles, information on sulfa and the Blitz and so much more. Elizabeth Bristowe supplied me with helpful details about Britain in 1940–41. She also spotted some of my mistakes.

Sheila Stephens read the manuscript and assured me I was on the right track. Her daughter Jenny helped me with research and made me taste Marmite. I, like Charlotte, was unimpressed.

Barbara Hehner was, as usual, a godsend to a blind author who is prone to making both glaring and tiny errors.

Dr. Helen Brown was extremely perceptive with her critical comments, enthusiasm and useful facts.

These folks also upheld me and kept me straight: the staff at the Guelph Public Library, George and Ethel Hindley, Betty Lou Clark, Pat McCraw, Jenny Rodd, Mary Hockin and Claire Mackay.

I am grateful, as well, to the authors of books not previously mentioned, that provided me not only with facts but with feelings: Geoff Bilson's *The Guests of War*, Hester Burton's *In Spite of All Terror* and P.L. Travers's *I Go By Land, I Go By Sea* — I read it when I was a teenager and it moved me and started me imagining what it must be like to be exiled from home because of a war.

Thank you, one and all.

Copyright © 2010 by Jean Little.

All rights reserved. Published by Scholastic Canada Ltd.
SCHOLASTIC and DEAR CANADA and logos are trademarks
and/or registered trademarks of Scholastic Inc.

Library and Archives Canada Cataloguing in Publication

Little, Jean, 1932-
Exiles from the war : the war guests diary of Charlotte Mary
Twiss / Jean Little.

(Dear Canada)
ISBN 978-0-545-98617-5

I. Title. II. Series: Dear Canada

PS8523 I77.E84 2009   jC813'.54   C2009-905479-5

ISBN 10 0-545-98617-6

No part of this publication may be reproduced or stored in a retrieval
system, or transmitted in any form or by any means, electronic,
mechanical, recording, or otherwise, without written permission of the
publisher, Scholastic Canada Ltd., 604 King St. W., Toronto, Ontario
M5V 1E1, Canada. In the case of photocopying or other
reprographic copying, a licence must be obtained from Access Copyright
(Canadian Copyright Licensing Agency), 1 Yonge Street, Suite 800, Toronto,
Ontario M5E 1E5 (1-800-893-5777).

6 5 4 3 2 1   Printed in Canada 114   10 11 12 13 14

The display type was set in Berkley Bold.
The text was set in ElectraLT Regular.

First printing January 2010

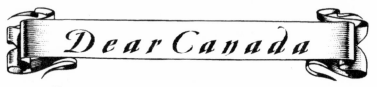
Dear Canada

Alone in an Untamed Land, The Filles du Roi Diary of Hélène St. Onge by Maxine Trottier

Banished from Our Home, The Acadian Diary of Angélique Richard by Sharon Stewart

Blood Upon Our Land, The North West Resistance Diary of Josephine Bouvier by Maxine Trottier

Brothers Far from Home, The World War I Diary of Eliza Bates by Jean Little

A Christmas to Remember, Tales of Comfort and Joy

Days of Toil and Tears, The Child Labour Diary of Flora Rutherford by Sarah Ellis

A Desperate Road to Freedom, The Underground Railroad Diary of Julia May Jackson by Karleen Bradford

The Death of My Country, The Plains of Abraham Diary of Geneviève Aubuchon by Maxine Trottier

Footsteps in the Snow, The Red River Diary of Isobel Scott by Carol Matas

If I Die Before I Wake, The Flu Epidemic Diary of Fiona Macgregor by Jean Little

No Safe Harbour, The Halifax Explosion Diary of Charlotte Blackburn by Julie Lawson

Not a Nickel to Spare, The Great Depression Diary of Sally Cohen by Perry Nodelman

An Ocean Apart, The Gold Mountain Diary of Chin Mei-ling by Gillian Chan

Orphan at My Door, The Home Child Diary of Victoria Cope
by Jean Little

*A Prairie as Wide as the Sea, The Immigrant Diary
of Ivy Weatherall* by Sarah Ellis

*Prisoners in the Promised Land, The Ukrainian Internment
Diary of Anya Soloniuk* by Marsha Skrypuch

*A Rebel's Daughter, The 1837 Rebellion Diary
of Arabella Stevenson* by Janet Lunn

*A Ribbon of Shining Steel, The Railway Diary of Kate
Cameron* by Julie Lawson

A Season for Miracles, Twelve Tales of Christmas

*A Trail of Broken Dreams, The Gold Rush Diary
of Harriet Palmer* by Barbara Haworth-Attard

*Turned Away, The World War II Diary
of Devorah Bernstein* by Carol Matas

*Where the River Takes Me, The Hudson's Bay Company Diary
of Jenna Sinclair* by Julie Lawson

Whispers of War, The War of 1812 Diary of Susanna Merritt
by Kit Pearson

*Winter of Peril, The Newfoundland Diary
of Sophie Loveridge* by Jan Andrews

*With Nothing But Our Courage, The Loyalist Diary
of Mary MacDonald* by Karleen Bradford

Go to www.scholastic.ca/dearcanada for information on the
Dear Canada Series — see inside the books, read an excerpt or
a review, post a review, and more.